Reunited

by Felice Stevens

Reunited (A Rescued Heart, Book 2)
January 2017

Print Edition

Cover Art by: Reese Dante www.reesedante.com
Licensed material is being used for illustrated purposes only and any person depicted in the licensed material is a model.

Edited by Keren Reed

Copyediting and proofreading provided by Flat Earth Editing.
www.flatearthediting.com

Published in the United States of America

Ryder Daniels and Jason Mallory seem to have it all but even the most loving marriage takes work. Ryder's past leads him to remain silent yet resentful in the face of conflict while Jason strives to prove he can take care of his family without Ryder's wealth, even if it costs him precious time with his husband and daughter.

When a devastating illness leaves them shaken and helpless, Ryder is forced to face the one person he never thought to see again with a life or death request that even he isn't sure will be granted, but his decisions have far-reaching consequences. Believing he and Ryder have no secrets, Jason is distraught to discover otherwise, revealing yet another crack in their once-perfect relationship.

Adrift and uncertain, both struggle to hold onto a love previously thought unshakeable. A forbidden past is exposed, shocking Ryder to the core, but it means little without Jason by his side. Marriage is a partnership and both men must learn that only by working through their pain and heartbreak together can they achieve a lifetime of love.

Dedication

To my family, now and forever.

Acknowledgments

As always, first thanks to my editor, Keren Reed. Thanks to Hope and Jessica from Flat Earth Editing for their help. I hope all the readers who've loved Ryder, Jason and the rest of the gang enjoy the conclusion to their story. And yes, I will be writing John's story, so keep tuned.

To the readers who've been with me since the beginning and those who are finding me now, thank you for your amazing support. Without you all, the ride wouldn't be half as sweet. Love you all to the moon and back.

For sneak peeks of WIP, exclusive content and other surprises, join my newsletter. No spam ever!
Newsletter: http://bit.ly/FelicesNewsletter

Chapter One

THE WEEK HAD dragged its ass so badly Jason Mallory could hardly believe Friday had finally arrived. He dug his phone out from the back pocket of his jeans and groaned. *For fuck's sake.* It felt like he'd been here forever, yet it was only eleven a.m. With longing he thought of the weekend, especially Sunday afternoon when, as usual, he'd be ensconced in a chair in the backyard of his parents' house, beer in hand. Wistfully, he stared at the picture of Ryder, their daughter, Gemma, and their two dogs, taken last year at Ryder's father's house in the Hamptons.

"Damn. We haven't been to the beach all summer."

Not that he could really complain. Mallory Brothers Construction had benefited from the boom in the real-estate market, and they could hardly keep up with the condo conversions and reno jobs they'd contracted. Only…Jason touched the phone screen with his finger. He missed out on dinnertimes with Gemma, listening to her chatter about her day, and then relaxing with Ryder after they put her to bed. The long days had been hell, even if the money was coming in.

As if by magic, the phone buzzed with a call from Ryder.

"Hey, babe."

"Hey. Are you busy?"

Jason could hear dogs barking in the background. "Are you at Rescue Me or out on a job? I don't recognize those barks."

"Yeah, we're coming back from a rescue in Fort Greene. Two dogs tied to a post in a yard for days. No food or water. I'd kill the bastards who did this if I ever found them. We're on our way to the vet now."

Anger simmered in Ryder's voice; Jason knew how personally he took these rescues. "Are they going to be okay?"

"Not sure. One is pretty bad off. Connor's already alerted Animal Care and Control to expect us. But that's not the reason I'm calling."

"Oh no? I bet I can guess." He dropped his voice low, in case any of his crew might walk by. The last thing they needed to hear was him talking dirty to his husband. "You miss my sexy ass. Or should I say, your dick in my ass like it was last night."

"Jesus." Ryder sucked in his breath, and Jason laughed at the thought of Ryder having to keep it cool with his best friend, Connor, sitting next to him.

"What? I'm wrong?" Jason sat down on the edge of a stone landing and cupped the phone to his mouth. "I can still feel you inside me, you know? And I want you again—first in the shower, all wet and soapy, then me inside you, holding you down on the bed. What do you say?"

"I can't really answer that the way I'd like to right now." The strain in Ryder's voice had Jason chuckling, then laughing out loud when he heard Connor yelling in the background.

"Jase. Are you having phone sex? No fair. I need it on speaker."

"How does he know what I'm saying?"

" 'Cause the bastard's got fucking Superman hearing or something."

"Liar," he heard Connor say cheerfully. "He got all red in the face and shifted away from me in the seat; that's how. You know Ryder can't hide shit from me."

That was the truth. Connor could sniff out anything—lies, half-truths, or embarrassing details. Nothing was safe from his inquisitive mind.

"Okay, calm down; I was only joking with you. What's up, Ry?" He eyed the group of workers setting the brickface on the façade of a row of townhouses they'd been renovating for weeks "Hold on a sec. Hey, Miguel! Watch that the cement isn't in the sun. It's gonna dry out quicker."

At his foreman's nod, he returned to Ryder. "Sorry. What were you saying?"

"I was thinking we could go away this weekend. Go to the Hamptons. I know it's last minute, but…"

"Damn, my mom is expecting us this weekend, Ry.

She's planning a big barbecue 'cause Liam and Courtney are coming by with the baby and everything."

"Oh. Couldn't we miss it just this once? You know I love going there, but I was thinking—"

"Aw, we can't. She really wants us to be there. You know how much she's been looking forward to having us all together. And now that Courtney's recovered, it'll be the first time TJ will be over."

A sigh escaped Ryder. "Come on, Jase. He's a newborn. He won't know where he is, and I'm sure your mom won't mind. I thought we could get away and lie around the beach. The summer's over, so it'll be nice and quiet. My dad and Denise won't be there; it'll just be us." His voice dropped. "You can do everything you mentioned before and more to me if you want."

Momentarily excited, Jason knew he'd have to refuse, no matter how tempting a weekend away at the beach sounded. Jason thought back to the phone call from his mother and how eagerly she'd been anticipating having Liam and Courtney over with the baby, and he didn't have the heart to disappoint her. Sunday night family times were so important to his parents, and he'd made the ritual as important to himself. With Nicole in her final year of law school in Boston and Jessie still in college, he and Ryder, along with Liam, had made certain to keep up the family tradition.

He'd always imagined having his family together for big dinners, kids running around, lots of laughter...buying the house, marrying Ryder, and having

Gemma were all part of that dream.

Not having a normal childhood, Ryder couldn't understand the concept of family weekends and togetherness. It made the difference between a house and a home, and all of Jason's hard work and time away from his family was for the sole purpose of creating a home for his family. Nothing was more important than them.

"Can we do it another weekend? It's not like you rented a house or anything. Your dad wouldn't mind us using it anytime; he's told me that."

"I know, but—"

Jason cast an approving eye over the brickwork his guys had begun laying, then he remembered he had to check in with Liam about the plans for the condo renovation in Long Island City and whether they'd received the City Building permits.

"Listen, I gotta go. I'll see you tonight. Don't hold dinner up for me; I'm gonna be late. Love you."

He hung up without waiting for Ryder's response and immediately dialed the Department of Buildings, his mind already on the next job. Hopefully he wouldn't be too tired when he got home later, and he could make it up to Ryder in other ways.

"DAMN." RYDER SHOVED the phone into his pocket and stared out of the van window, watching the other cars race past them on the road.

"What's the matter? Jason said no?" With the practiced ease of someone used to New York City traffic, Connor steered the van past the double-parked delivery trucks on East 92nd St. He pulled into a No Standing zone and flipped over the parking pass the ASPCA had given them.

Remaining seated, Ryder fingered his wedding ring. "Yeah. It's no big deal." He mustered a halfhearted smile. "He promised his mom we'd be there." At the sight of Connor taking a breath, Ryder put up his hand. "Don't. I know what you're going to say. But he's right. It's not like we can't do it another weekend. We will, and I feel badly about disappointing his mom, too. She's been like a mother to me."

He unbuckled his seat belt and left the van, meeting Connor in the back. Together they lifted the two crates carrying the dogs, and with help from the assistants who'd come running outside when they'd pulled up, they carried them inside. Filling out the paperwork took only a few minutes, and he and Connor finished up, with assurances that they'd be informed if the dogs were adopted. With one last pat to each of the dogs, Ryder and Connor left them in the care of the very capable veterinarians and walked outside.

"Want to grab something before heading back? I could use a little walk and some coffee." Connor rubbed his stomach. "Emily has me on a diet."

At Connor's woeful expression, Ryder grinned. "I shouldn't aid and abet you but I wouldn't mind a snack."

They headed west up 92nd St., walking in silence until they hit a diner.

"This looks good, right?"

The once-ubiquitous New York City diner was fading fast, replaced by high-priced coffee chains and grab-and-go salad and sandwich places. He nodded and followed Connor inside.

"Anywhere you want, boys; I'll be right over." The harried waitress tipped her head to the left, and he and Connor walked over and slid into a booth.

"Are you going to let me speak now, or will you keep deflecting me like you always do?"

"Not like I could stop you anyway," Ryder muttered.

"You should talk to your husband like you talk to me."

"What the hell does that mean?" Ryder shot back, ready to argue but he spotted the waitress advancing on their table and held off.

"What can I get you guys? Coffee?" The aroma from the pot she carried smelled heavenly.

"For me, yes. Thanks." Ryder slid his cup over. "I'll take a toasted corn muffin too, please."

"Coffee for me please." Connor smiled up at the waitress "And a cherry danish."

The waitress finished pouring their coffees and left, at which point Ryder quirked a brow.

"Cherry danish? Emily will be pissed at you."

"She won't know unless you rat me out. Which you won't because you're my best friend."

Connor took a sip of his coffee. "And you're doing it again. Turning the conversation away from yourself and your problem."

"I don't have any problems. I'm happy. See?" He poured milk into his coffee and beamed a toothpaste-commercial-worthy smile at Connor, who remained unimpressed.

"Bullshit. You constantly let Jason walk all over you. Look what happened right before, in the van. Why couldn't you tell him you'd planned a surprise for him this weekend? You know he would've jumped on it, and I told you Emily and I are happy to take Gemma and let you two have the weekend to yourselves."

Annoyed with himself and with Connor for calling him out, Ryder frowned into the milky depths of his coffee. "I…I don't let him walk all over me. I understand his mom wants everyone together 'cause it'll be TJ's first time there. These family occasions mean everything to her." Catching a glimpse of Connor's dubious expression, Ryder prayed for the waitress to come back. What took so long for a corn muffin, damn it? "What do I know about family traditions?"

"Come on, Ry, that's BS and you know it. And it isn't only this. You're always backing down, giving Jason the say-so in everything—whenever you go to the movies, it's his choice, or on vacations, it's always with his family. When was the last time you told him you wanted something and didn't back down if he disagreed?"

"I love Jason, and it makes him happy to spend time with his family. I love them too."

At last the waitress approached with their plates, and Ryder could busy himself with buttering his muffin and not have to face Connor's piercing stare.

"I love Jason too, and frankly this isn't his problem, it's yours. If Emily would agree with everything I said all the time, I'd be happy too and not complain."

"You'd be dead or dreaming 'cause that would never happen."

"Exactly." Connor took half of his corn muffin.

"Give that back."

"Then pay attention to me and take what I'm saying seriously."

Ryder let out a laugh. "Are you holding my corn muffin hostage?"

Connor's smile faded. "Ry. You don't have to do that, you know. Jason loves you. You guys can disagree and it will still be okay."

Ryder chewed on the other half of his muffin. "Uh-huh." He understood, really he did. But why make waves?

Chapter Two

"DADDY!"

Four-year-old Gemma's plaintive cry split the night. Ryder squinted at the glowing numbers on the digital clock next to his bed. Three a.m. *Shit.* Nothing good ever happened at this hour of the night, or morning, if he wanted to get technical. Maybe it was a bad dream, even though Gemma rarely woke up at night anymore.

He settled down beneath the warmth of the comforter, preparing to fall back asleep. Jason moved closer to him, and Ryder slid his foot down Jason's calf, relishing the scrape of his hairy leg. As long as he was up, it shouldn't be a total loss. Ryder kissed Jason's naked shoulder and licked up his strong neck, the steady pulse of life quickening beneath his lips. Jason's sighs spurred him on, and Ryder smiled to himself, unsure whether his husband was fully awake, but that didn't stop him from palming Jason's ass and giving it a hard squeeze.

"Daddy, please. Come."

Damn. No use. Fully awake now, Ryder slid out of bed, immediately missing Jason's solid heat. Longingly he gazed back down at him splayed out in the center of the bed and shook his head with dismay. The man worked too damn hard. Jason had collapsed after they put Gemma to sleep the night before, barely able to stifle his yawns long enough to eat dinner. Mallory Brothers Construction had taken off in the past few years, and though Jason and Liam had hired several other architects and construction engineers to help alleviate the load of work they took on, Jason still tried to be as hands-on as possible. He and Ryder had numerous discussions about his long hours and how they kept him from being home with Gemma, but Jason insisted his presence was necessary, and Ryder backed off, unwilling to argue about it.

The past few weeks, Ryder tried to push dinner later and later, but Gemma had fallen asleep at the dinner table too many times for that to remain feasible. He loved the quiet times at night when they'd sit together and he'd read her a bedtime story, but Ryder missed having Jason beside him, sharing those special moments. The last thing Ryder wanted was for Jason to work so hard he missed Gemma's childhood; his own father had missed his and Landon's childhoods by burying himself in his work. Ryder wouldn't allow Jason to do that, but he had to find a way to tell Jason without him getting upset.

"What's wrong?" Jason mumbled, his face buried in

the pillow. "I had a dream someone was copping a feel." He turned his cheek on the pillow and mustered a tired smile. "Thought I was gonna get lucky."

"You were about to, but Gemma woke up before I could make your dreams come true. Go back to sleep, babe." Ryder leaned down to kiss Jason's stubble-rough cheek. "She probably had a bad dream."

"Mmm. Well, hurry back. I was dreaming of the beach, and you were my hot cabana boy." He wiggled his ass. "I'm ready for my massage."

Ryder snorted and rolled his eyes. "You're insane." But he couldn't help kissing Jason's smooth shoulder again. "Be right back," he whispered against Jason's skin, but all he received was an answering sleepy sigh.

Pearl and Trouper waited outside the bedroom door, ridiculously bright-eyed and awake for the middle of the night. Both dogs kept him company, trailing behind him on his trek down the hall.

He pushed open the half-closed door to Gemma's room, and even though she'd woken him up out of a deep sleep, Ryder couldn't help but smile at the sight of her sitting up in her little toddler bed, rubbing her eyes. Gemma had been so proud when she'd graduated from her crib and insisted on picking out the bedding. Naturally, dogs played a big part in the design. Her numerous stuffed animals slept with her every night, surrounding her like a fuzzy zoo.

"Hi, baby girl."

"Not a baby, Daddy." She pouted, and Ryder

watched her round eyes fill with tears. "My head hurts and I feel funny."

The dogs padded over to her and pushed their faces onto her mattress, whining slightly until she petted them. Ryder crossed the room and knelt at her bedside. It was unusual for her to complain; Gemma rarely even caught a cold, but she had seemed unusually tired lately, which he'd chalked up to excitement over starting preschool a few weeks ago.

"Funny how? Funny like throw-up funny, or funny another way?" He smoothed his hands over her strawberry-blonde curls, resting his fingers along her soft cheeks, relieved she had no fever at least. It never ceased to fill him with wonder that his and Jason's love had contributed to the creation of this little person, and her life was their responsibility. Ryder loved Gemma so much it hurt his heart sometimes simply to look at her.

"Funny like things are all spinny and I feel sick." A fat little tear escaped to roll down her cheek. "I'm scared." She hiccupped a short breath.

Ryder sat on the shaggy rug next to her bed and patted the mattress next to her. "How about you lie down, and I stay right here and tell you a story until you fall back asleep. But if you still don't feel well in the morning, we'll have to take you to see the doctor. How's that?"

Yawning, she nodded. "Okay." She lay down, and he covered her with her fluffy purple comforter and kissed her forehead. Without opening her eyes, she spoke. "I want Pearl and Trouper to stay too."

At the sound of their names, they gave gruff little barks and lay down next to Ryder, like two large sentinels. Ryder couldn't help but laugh; both huge dogs became nothing but putty in Gemma's hands. From the moment he and Jason brought her home from the hospital, Pearl and Trouper made Gemma their priority, as if they knew how special she was. Wherever she could be found, they were with her, and Ryder couldn't be sure who loved whom more.

"Of course. All three of us."

"I wanna hear how you met Daddy Jay."

"You've heard that story a hundred times." Smiling, Ryder stretched out his legs. "Aren't you tired of it?"

"Please?" She let out a huge yawn. " 'Cause it has Trouper in it."

How could he resist? "Okay. Aunt Emily and I got a call from your uncle Liam, who said they'd found some dogs when he and Daddy Jay were working on some buildings. I was still working full-time at Rescue Me then, and Aunt Em and I went to see what we could do to help."

"And Daddy Jay thought you and Aunt Emily were married. That's so funny." Gemma let out a little giggle.

It was. Ryder would never forget seeing Jason for the first time, standing in his work clothes in the parking lot of his construction site. When their eyes met, their immediate, electric connection rocked him to the core. He'd never experienced that with anyone, and from that moment on, Ryder's life had changed forever.

"It was. And then I found the dogs, including Trouper, who was a little puppy, and we brought them back to the rescue. A few days later Daddy Jay called and wanted to adopt Trouper."

"Trouper and Pearl are best friends like me and Shanice." Her eyelids fluttered closed. "Shanice is coming to play on Sunday, Erica said."

Erica, their housekeeper and sometimes babysitter, had been with them since Gemma's birth. When Ryder and Jason discovered she would have to put her own child in daycare to work for them, they insisted she bring little Shanice with her. And when Gemma was ready to start preschool they secured Shanice a place as well. The two little girls became inseparable. Ryder couldn't stop laughing when Shanice shyly told him that Gemma had "lent" one of her daddies to her for Father/Daughter day at school, since Shanice's father had died when she was only a baby.

"That's nice. Maybe we can all go to the park."

"Okay." Gemma yawned again and closed her eyes. Her even breathing after a few minutes had passed indicated she'd fallen asleep at last. Ryder glanced down at Pearl, who gazed back at him with intelligent eyes, her tail wagging furiously against the rug. "You want to stay here with her?" Trouper had already planted himself on the opposite side of the bed, resting his muzzle on the mattress. He hadn't taken his eyes off Gemma.

With a whine, Pearl licked his hand, and Ryder scratched her head. "Okay, girl. You and Troup watch over her and come get me if she wakes up again." He received an answering lick, then Pearl circled the rug and sprawled out, settling in for the night.

Careful to keep quiet, Ryder walked on the balls of his feet, leaving the door halfway open on his way out. Back in his bedroom, the illuminated dial of the clock shone out as 3:37. Sighing, he slipped back into bed.

"Ry?" Jason cracked open one eye. "What was wrong?"

Ryder settled under the comforter, relishing the feel of Jason's warm feet tangling with his cold ones. "Gem said she had a headache and felt funny. Luckily she fell back asleep pretty quickly. Pearl and Trouper are keeping her company." He slid closer to Jason and grinned at the feel of his husband's erection through the thin sweatpants they'd both taken to wearing to bed since Gemma had grown big enough to climb out of her crib and come to their bedroom. "I see you missed me."

"Huh. Must be that hot cabana boy I was dreaming about. Funny though, he looked like you." The low chuckle in his ear was followed by Jason nuzzling the side of his neck. "All my sexy dreams involve you. Get closer." Jason sucked at his neck and desire flooded through Ryder as all thoughts of sleep fled.

Though they'd been married over five years, his passion for Jason remained as fresh as the first time Ryder touched him. He couldn't imagine a time when the sight of Jason wouldn't thrill him. Ryder flipped back the covers and with a sureness born of practice, hooked his fingers onto Jason's sweats and yanked them down, revealing his husband's heavy cock.

"So, waking up shouldn't be a total loss at this god-forsaken time of night..." Ryder bent down and took Jason deep into his mouth, his tongue flattening around the thick base of Jason's cock. The smell and taste of Jason fed his soul like the warmth of summer. He could never get enough of this man.

"Fuck yeah," Jason groaned, falling back on the pillows.

Ryder hummed, licking up and down Jason's rigid length, lightly circling the head with his tongue before flicking at the slit, already wet with Jason's precome. He engulfed Jason's cock fully, creating the wet suction he knew Jason craved. By the pleading sounds escaping his husband's lips and the frantic bucking of his hips, Ryder could tell Jason's climax wasn't far off.

With the wet tips of his fingers, Ryder teased at Jason's hole, sinking two fingers deep inside his ass. He curled his fingers upward, listening to and loving the desperate, greedy sounds escaping Jason's lips. From the first, Jason had been a demonstrative lover, and Ryder relished every groan and gasp. He pumped his fingers harder and faster, instinctively knowing the right places to touch to bring Jason the greatest amount of pleasure.

"Fuck, Ry." Jason convulsed underneath Ryder, exploding in his mouth, his salty essence sliding down

Ryder's throat. He stiffened then shuddered to completion. Ryder drank him down, then withdrew his fingers, sat up, and wiped his mouth, smiling at the blissful expression plastered on Jason's face.

"Feel good, babe?"

Without opening his eyes, Jason held out his hand, and Ryder took it, lacing their fingers together. He curled up next to Jason, burrowing back under the covers next to him. Jason's warmth soaked through him, chasing away the nighttime chill.

"It's always good, Ry. I always feel good with you."

Jason lay still for a moment, and Ryder noticed his brow furrowed as if he were troubled.

"What's wrong?"

Jason let go of Ryder's hand to pull up his sweats. "I just remembered last week Gemma also said her head hurt. I didn't think much of it, but now she's complaining about it again, bad enough that it woke her up."

A thin trickle of dread wiggled through Ryder. "We should call the doctor in the morning, then." He lay on his side facing Jason, all thoughts of his own pleasure vanishing.

"Let's see how she feels when she wakes up. If she's perfectly fine, we can watch her. How about I ask my mom what she thinks?" Jason slid his leg over Ryder, forcing their bodies close. "She raised the five of us and must've seen everything."

"You don't think anything's wrong, do you?" Ryder sank into Jason's muscled chest and wrapped his arms around him, swallowing down his fear. Jason held him close, and only then did his nerves quiet. The steady, sure beat of Jason's heart thumped in his ear. It was the music he fell asleep to every night and what he woke up to in the morning, playing in his head.

"Nah. She probably overdid it at the park with Jack and Emily. You know how she likes to think she can keep up with him even though he's two years older."

At that Ryder laughed, the image of Gemma's chubby legs running after Connor and Emily's six-year-old son, Jack, banishing further worry from his mind. They had all thought Gemma would want to play with the new baby, Isabel, but she preferred to be with Jack, which annoyed the boy to no end. Hence his running away from Gemma every chance he got.

"You're probably right." Ryder kissed Jason, their tongues sliding and tangling as they leisurely explored each other's mouths. Jason could steal his soul, the breath from his body, and Ryder wouldn't care; he'd willingly give it up to him. "I love you, you know?"

Jason pulled him nearer, his strong arms holding him close. "I might have suspected. Love you too. We'll call my mom in the morning. But she's eating okay and looks good. Let's try and get some sleep."

Ryder held on tight to Jason and closed his eyes. Helen would know what to do; Jason was right. She'd seen everything and would know best. It was probably nothing at all.

Chapter Three

"MA, I TOLD you, I only know these two times. Other than that she seems fine." Jason rolled his eyes at Ryder, who grinned and gave him a wink. He gripped the phone. "We'll come by later today."

"I want you to come this morning before she gets too tired and needs her nap. When I saw her last weekend she was a little cranky, but I put that down to her missing her afternoon nap."

"We'll be there by noon, how's that?" Saturday mornings were made for leisurely breakfasts with Ryder and Gemma. He looked forward to it all week. With a sigh of contentment, he sipped his coffee.

"Perfect. Courtney said TJ smiled at her this morning." His mother's voice rang full with pride. Jason knew there was nothing she loved more than having all her family and grandchildren around. Now that Liam and Courtney had their baby, his mother was the happiest woman on earth.

"Great, I can't wait to see them." He and Ryder had visited the hospital when Courtney had the baby, a little boy they named Anthony after Jason's father, but whom everyone called Tony Jr. or TJ.

After hanging up the phone, he turned to Ryder, who, with Gemma at the stove, busily made what was supposed to be breakfast. From their conversation it looked like pancakes, although what was on the plate in no way bore a resemblance to any excuse for a pancake Jason had ever seen. Doused with enough syrup and fruit on top, Jason would eat it. Damn, he'd eat nails for Gemma. That little girl had his heart in such a vise-like grip she might as well take it and wear it inside her own body. Sometimes Jason woke up at night and went into her bedroom to simply watch her sleep; he counted his blessings for a life so full of love and happiness it scared him sometimes.

He wanted to give Gemma everything—the world if he could. Ryder grew frustrated at every additional project he took on, but Jason couldn't let Ryder know of the gnawing anxiety inside that he could never measure up to the lifestyle Ryder came from. Instead, he minimized Ryder's objections to his long hours by ignoring them. Childish, yeah, but Ryder had stopped asking, so Jason let it slide. He knew Ryder wouldn't push him and took advantage of his husband's good nature. Jason promised himself—once these projects were done, he'd slow down and take on less work.

The only other problem he and Ryder had was their constant disagreement over Ryder's mother. No matter what the occasion, Ryder insisted on inviting her. And even though she never accepted, never called or even acknowledged Gemma's birth, Ryder stubbornly clung to the hope that one day she'd come around, simply because she was his mother.

"Daddy Jay, how many pancakes?"

Jason pushed all negative thoughts of Astrid Daniels out of his mind to concentrate on his daughter. She looked so cute in the NY Jets football jersey she'd insisted they buy her once she saw Jack wearing one at the park.

Um, none? But being the brave father he was, Jason smiled brightly at her and held up two fingers. "Two, baby."

She frowned. "I tole you. I'm not a baby. I'm a big girl."

He bit back a smile. "You're right. I'll take two, Miss Gemma, please."

With a very serious expression, she nodded and held up the plate to Ryder. "Daddy Jay wants two."

Ryder slid two misshapen excuses for pancakes on Jason's plate. "Okay, honey. Ask him what he wants with it, bacon or sausage."

Her face screwed up in concentration, Gemma walked slowly over to the table and placed a plate with something that was supposed to represent a stack of pancakes in front of him. "Daddy Ry wants to know if you want bacon or sausage."

Jason took the plate from her and kissed her cheek. "Tell him both."

As if Ryder couldn't hear, she turned around and yelled. "He wants both."

Ryder glanced over his shoulder and winked. "Both it is. Have to keep up your strength. You've been working hard day and night."

Heat flooded through Jason, remembering how Ryder had woken him up during the night and how he intended to repay the favor later after Gemma went to bed.

He sipped his coffee. "Mom said we should get there by noon."

Gemma's round blue eyes lit up. "Yay. I wanna see Nana and Poppy." She danced around the kitchen, and Pearl and Trouper barked and danced with her.

"No going to see anyone until you sit and eat breakfast, then take a bath."

"But I took one yesterday." She stuck out her lower lip and gazed at him with pleading eyes.

Gemma's adorable pouting didn't work. The last thing he wanted was to raise a bratty child, and he made a note to ask his mother for tips. That she'd raised him and his brothers and sisters and they'd all turned out pretty normal was a sign she knew exactly what to do. And it wasn't as if they could call Ryder's mother. Jason always wondered how Ryder and his brother turned out as loving as they did with an ice queen like Astrid Daniels for a mother.

"We've told you before; you need to take a bath every day."

Her eyes narrowed, and Jason couldn't help but notice how much she looked like Ryder.

"I want bubbles. Daddy Ry said I could yesterday, I remember."

And like her lawyer-father, Ryder, she'd become an excellent negotiator.

"Okay. Finish your breakfast, and then a big bubble bath before Nana and Poppy's house." He pointed to the chair. "Sit and I'll help you cut your pancakes." This had become his favorite part of the weekend, next to late Saturday nights and early Sunday mornings with Ryder in bed. Sitting with Gemma and hearing her talk about her week with her friends and all they did together made him realize how full his life was now compared to the emptiness of his twenties. Those long-ago years with his old girlfriend Chloe now seemed like they'd happened to a different person.

"Hey, you." Ryder put a plate of bacon and sausages between their seats. "You looked kind of serious there." He joined him and took a piece of bacon. "Everything okay?"

A tiny dart of fear jabbed Jason as he stared into Ryder's eyes. What would he do if he ever lost Ryder? The love between them hadn't dimmed in all their years together; their mutual passion remained electric, and the absolute joy of coming home to find Ryder and Gemma waiting for him at the dinner table exceeded any dreams he'd had of a home and family.

"I love you, you know?"

Ryder's eyes grew soft. "Yeah? I might have guessed"—his voice dropped down low—"especially after last night. I love you too. Something wrong?"

"Nothing. Just thinking."

And Ryder accepted his answer because their closeness meant they didn't always need to explain with words. Jason knew Ryder; he knew by his breathing if he hurt and by the pace of his heartbeat when he was happy. They were part of each other's blood and bones. Their life had settled into a contented pattern of raising Gemma, taking care of their dogs, their jobs, friends, and family. Nothing else mattered to Jason. He had everything he'd ever wanted.

"Daddy Jay, I finished my pancakes. Can I take my bubble bath now?" Having no concept of personal space, she stuck her face in his and patted his cheek. "Can you come with me?"

Ryder nudged him. "Go ahead. You haven't had alone time with her in a while, since you've been working so hard. I'll clean up here."

"I do it for us, you know that, right? It won't always be this way."

Without meeting his eyes, Ryder busied himself with the plates. "Sure, go on with Gemma."

It took him only a minute to shove the rest of his pancakes in his mouth and wash them down with a cup of coffee. "Okay, baby girl. Let's go." He picked her up and put her on his shoulders, setting her off squealing with laughter.

Before leaving the table, he kissed the top of Ryder's silky head. "I'll do the same for you tonight." Meeting Ryder's heated gaze, he gave a wicked grin. "If you're a good boy, that is."

"I'm always good. Great, in fact." Ryder's return smile shone equally wicked and sexy-sweet, and suddenly Jason wished they didn't have to go to his parents' and could spend the day together.

"Don't I know it."

"Let's go, Daddy Jay." She bounced up and down on his shoulders. "I want bubbles. I want bubbles."

"Good God. We need to give this child less sugar. Calm down, Gem. We're going." Followed by the two dogs as usual, Jason continued to bounce Gemma on his shoulders as he walked up the stairs to the bathroom next to Gemma's room. With great care, he picked her up off his shoulders and snuggled her close. "I love you, baby girl."

"Me too." Her cool, smooth cheek pressed against his.

"Go pick out your outfit and come back in to take your bath. I'll start the water."

"Okay." She ran off into her bedroom, Trouper scrabbling after her. Pearl sat with him, and he stroked her silky ears.

"How're you doing, girl? I miss playing with you guys too. We'll take you and Troup to the park tomorrow." He scratched behind her ear, and she licked his face. There was something so stress relieving about

Pearl. Knowing how she'd helped Ryder through the worst of times made her extra special to him. One of the reasons Ryder had remained as sane as he did during his breakup with an old boyfriend and the estrangement from his bitch of a mother was this dog, and for that Jason would do anything for her.

Clothes in hand, Gemma entered the bathroom in her purple, fuzzy robe and blue slippers, her faithful bodyguard Trouper right at her heels. "I'm ready for my bath."

Jason took the jeans and T-shirt from her and put them on the shelf behind him so they wouldn't get wet. She took off her robe and got into the tub, and he poured in a capful of bubbles. Soon she sat splashing in the iridescent foam and looked so cute he couldn't help take a poof of the bubbles and dot her nose with it.

"Here's your washcloth. Don't forget to scrub your face and behind your ears."

Giving him as reproachful a look as only a child could, Gemma dipped the cloth in the water and washed her face. "I know what to do. I take a bath every day, but you're not here." The washcloth dropped into the bathtub and floated on the surface. "Why do you haveta work so late? Daddy Ry and me miss you. He always looks sad when we have dinner by ourselves."

Jason's heart squeezed tightly. "Your uncle Liam and I have a lot of new buildings we're working on. I'm trying to make money for our future so you can go to a good school and we can give you everything you need."

"You don't have to do that; I've told you already."

Hearing Ryder's quiet voice behind him, Jason's heart plummeted. He picked up the washcloth and handed it back to Gemma before turning around to face his husband.

"No, what you told me was we don't have to worry because you have enough money in your trust fund. I'm not taking money from your mother. You know that." He so didn't want to hear this right now.

Ryder sank down next to him and let the water drain out of the tub, then turned on the taps to allow fresh water for Gemma to rinse off. "It's not her money. I've told you my trust fund comes from my grandmother."

It frustrated Jason no end to have to explain this to Ryder. After such a long time, he thought this topic of conversation had been discussed to death and settled. It certainly had in his mind at least.

"I know. But it's an extension of her. I'm cool with your father and love him, and I know he loves Gemma, but still…I can provide for my family—we both can. You and I make do on our own without needing help from anyone."

They finished drying off Gemma and dressed her in her jeans and T-shirt.

"Go ahead to your room until we're ready to go, okay?" Ryder gave her a kiss on the cheek. "Daddy Jay and I will clean up in here."

"You don't look happy." Serious blue eyes flitted

between his and Ryder's. "You're not gonna have a fight, are you?"

"Of course not. Go on." Ryder swatted her behind, and she left, but not before shooting dubious looks over her shoulder.

"I don't understand," said Ryder as he rinsed out the tub. "I'm the one wronged by my mother, and I have no problem with my grandmother's money. She loved me. And whether or not she knew I was gay when she was alive is irrelevant now. If I can use her money to make life easier for my family, I don't see why it bothers you so much."

Growing up rich, Ryder never had to think twice about paying bills or getting what he wanted. But Jason didn't come from that background. Working-class and cognizant of the cost of everything from food to schooling, Jason refused to succumb to the temptation of allowing Ryder's money to take care of all their expenses. Gemma would not grow up to be a spoiled, self-entitled girl if he had his way.

"Aren't I enough?" Jason hunkered down on his heels next to Ryder by the bathtub. "I think we do fine on our own, and I don't want your mother or anyone thinking they have a hold over me or telling me how to raise my child. Or that I don't contribute enough to our family."

"Babe, that's crazy." Ryder's warm palm slid across Jason's face to settle at the nape of his neck. "There'd be no family without you. It only makes sense because we're doing this together. You, me, and Gemma. A family unit."

Mollified, Jason nuzzled into Ryder's neck. "I love you guys so much. I don't want you to ever think you made a mistake, or that I'm not enough."

"Not enough? You're everything I ever wanted. You and Gemma. I sometimes get so scared thinking where I'd be if I didn't have you. We'll figure it out like we always do." Ryder pulled him close. "Together."

Jason wrapped his arms around Ryder and held him close, satisfied that he'd been foolish to allow the distractions in his head to override his heart. He didn't need to prove himself. Ryder loved him, and that was all Jason needed. "I want it to be only us—you and me—taking care of Gemma. I don't want to rely on anyone else. I've seen enough of how money can ruin kids, and I won't let that happen to her. I've been paying my own way since college. Gemma might not have the fanciest clothes, but she'll know she's loved, and that's something money can't buy."

Ryder stiffened and pulled away. "Wait a minute. I'm not a bad person because I came from money. Money, or the lack of it, doesn't make a person kind or generous. It's what you choose to do with your life. Look around the city at all the museums, libraries, and parks. If it wasn't for rich people giving their time and money, none of that would exist."

"I didn't mean—"

Ryder didn't get angry often, but when he did, the

lawyer in him came out and he wouldn't back down until he had his say. "Yeah, you did. Are we supposed to ask a parent's net worth before Gemma's allowed to be friends with their child? Damn. I never knew you resented me so much."

This argument was fast cycling out of control. Frustrated, Jason stood and blocked the doorway to make sure Ryder didn't walk away without them hashing this out to the end. "You're being ridiculous. I don't resent you. I love you. You aren't that type of person I'm talking about, you or Landon. Neither is your father now that I've gotten to know him. Yeah, I prejudged him in the beginning but only because of how badly I felt he treated you. But I don't want your mother to have the slightest bit of influence over Gemma, and taking her money, whether it was from your grandmother or directly from her, makes me feel like she's a part of our lives."

Ryder blew out a breath. "What would happen if she ever came to me and apologized for everything she did and said, not only to me but you as well? You still think I should turn her away?"

That ludicrous scenario almost made him laugh, but Ryder would never forgive him if he so much as cracked a smile. That woman would sooner walk naked down Park Avenue than acknowledge Jason and apologize to him. "Babe, I hate to tell you this, but it's never going to happen. And why do you keep doing it? Why do you want her in your life when she's been nothing but horrible to you?"

A somber expression settled on Ryder's face. "I don't know." His eyes took on a faraway look. "Maybe I'm stupid and still believe there's good in everyone. And even if she hates me, I still can't believe she knows she has a granddaughter and won't acknowledge her existence. Some outside influence must be preventing her. She'd love Gemma, I'm certain of it."

Personally, Jason thought Ryder saw what he wanted to see and was fooling himself. Jason couldn't imagine that cold witch ever loving anyone but herself. "Guess if that day comes where she wants to see Gem, we'll discuss it." Never would be too soon for Jason if it meant being in the presence of Astrid Daniels. Ryder attempted to pass by him, and Jason grabbed hold of his arm. "I'm sorry if I upset you. I'd never stand in your way if she came to you, you know that."

Keeping his gaze on the floor, Ryder shrugged and scuffed his sneaker on the marble threshold of the bathroom. "I know it won't happen. But it's hard to have Gemma ask me about my family and explain why she's never met her other grandmother. I love your mom, she's the best, but it's like there's something inside me pushing me to find out why my mother became who she is today."

Still holding Ryder's arm, he turned him so that they faced each other. "Let's get Gemma ready to go see my parents. We'll figure out everything together. Okay?" He squeezed Ryder's arm.

Ryder gave him a quick smile which, to Jason's relief, now reached his eyes. "I'm ready when you are."

"We're good, right?" Jason pressed. The one thing he didn't want was for an argument to linger between them.

"Yeah. I'll get Gemma downstairs while you get the dogs ready."

"Sounds good." Jason gave Ryder's arm another squeeze then headed downstairs. He whistled for the dogs, and within seconds he heard them tearing down the stairs, their tags jingling. They jumped around his feet, tongues lolling and tails wagging like furious metronomes.

"Settle down, you two." He snapped on their leashes and took the ends in one hand as Ryder came down the steps with Gemma in tow. "We all set?"

Gemma held up her knapsack. "I have all my stickers and stuff. Nana said she'd make a story with me."

"Sounds like fun. Let's go, then."

They dealt with their jackets and Gemma's and finally made it out the door with the dogs straining on their leads. Ryder buckled Gemma into her car seat, and the dogs jumped into the back seat, one on either side of her. He slid behind the wheel and waited for Ryder to buckle himself in before starting the engine. The ride only took about ten minutes and before long, the familiar large brick and wood Victorian home came into sight. He pulled into the driveway behind Liam's car.

Between the dogs barking and Gemma chattering,

Jason longingly thought of the large peaceful backyard and a nice cold beer. It wouldn't be too hard for him and Ryder to steal away to find some quiet time together, and he made a mental note to sneak his husband away for a make-out session.

The double front doors opened, framing his mother's smiling face. Gemma let go of Ryder's hand and ran to her, yelling at the top of her lungs.

"Nana, Nana. I helped make the pancakes today."

So much for her not feeling well. Earlier that morning she hadn't exhibited any of the symptoms that had woken her up during the night or that she'd complained about earlier in the week. Maybe it was simply a bug she picked up at the park. Lord knows kids passed along enough of each other's germs. His mom scooped her up and smothered her with kisses. "You did? I'm so jealous I didn't get some. Maybe one time your daddies will let you sleep over, and you can make some for me and Poppy." She glanced over Gemma's bright strawberry-blonde curls and winked at him. He grinned back, knowing full well that her offer was for his and Ryder's benefit.

"Yes, please, can I, can I?" Gemma squirmed around to look at both of them.

"Yes."

He and Ryder spoke at the same time, then looked at each other and laughed.

"Not too eager, are we?" He nudged Ryder's shoulder, then got pulled away by the two dogs who, having spied the open door, anticipated freedom. He unclipped them from their leashes, and they tore inside.

"I'll take any alone time with you I can get," said Ryder. "You're so exhausted lately I hate waking you up in the morning."

"Jason? Ryder?" His mother's alarmed voice sounded from inside the house. "Come here."

Together they hurried inside, where Gemma stood in her T-shirt. Her little denim jacket lay at her feet.

"What's wrong, Mom?"

"Look at her shoulder by her neck—it's all bruised. There and there." His mother pointed out the dark spots on Gemma's skin. "And she has other bruises up and down her arms."

"She's always getting bumps and bruises, Mom. Every day she goes to the park, and between the slide and the jungle gym, she's bound to come away with them."

His mother's worried gaze met his. "I know, but this seems excessive to me. And you mentioned this morning how she wasn't feeling well last night. I think you should call the doctor and have her checked out."

At the mention of the word doctor, Gemma grabbed hold of his hand. "Nooo. I don't wanna go to the doctor. I'm fine."

He tried to give his mother a reassuring smile. "I think she's okay. It was probably one of those things kids give to each other in school. Here today and gone tomorrow."

"I don't know; she looks kind of pale to me," his mother demurred as she ran her hand over Gemma's forehead. "She doesn't have a fever."

"No, Daddy, I'm fine. I don't wanna go to the doctor." Gemma pulled on his hand. "I'm not sick."

Her eyes beamed bright, but maybe his mother was right. Maybe it was because she looked pale. "Let me see what you mean. I didn't notice anything on her when we gave her a bath before; did you, Ry?"

"No. Show me your arm, Gem."

Ryder hunkered down on his heels next to him and ran his fingers over Gemma's arm, which she obediently held out to him. "Does it hurt, honey?"

"No. I swear." She sniffled. "I bet it's the stupid car seat. I told you I don't need it anymore."

"Yes, you do, and it wouldn't make bruises on your arm. These seem to have sprung up from nowhere." He slid her jeans up her leg, exposing her calf. Several mottled bruises stood out like ugly purple marks against her fair skin. "These too. I don't get it. We literally took her from the bath to here, and I swear there was nothing before."

By now Gemma had had enough of their poking and prodding. "I wanna go see the baby. I wanna see TJ." Without waiting for an answer, she sprinted off down the hallway before he or Ryder could stop her.

"I don't like it, you two. Those bruises don't look good to me." His mother picked up Gemma's jacket and hung it on the newel post of the banister.

Alarmed, Jason glanced at Ryder, who gazed wide-eyed at his mother. "What should we do? It's the weekend, and her doctor doesn't have hours. Is it an emergency, or do you think it can wait until Monday?"

The three of them walked together toward the back of the house, to where Gemma had run off. They found her ensconced in Liam's lap, baby TJ cradled in his other arm. The baby had one of Gemma's fingers tight in his grasp, while Liam looked on with a satisfied smile.

"Hey, guys." Liam grinned. "I'd wave, but I'm a little full right now."

"He's so strong, Uncle Liam. TJ likes to hold my finger." Gemma glanced over at Ryder and him. "Look, Daddy Jay. TJ loves me."

"Of course he does, baby girl. Hey, Courtney, how are you feeling?"

He kissed his sister-in-law while Ryder greeted his father. TJ's birth had been difficult, and Courtney had needed to spend several nights in the hospital. Two months at home under both Liam's and his mother's care would cure anyone of their problems. Either that or she couldn't wait to escape.

"I'm good, thanks, but Jase, what's with the bruises on Gemma's arms?"

Liam let out a shout before he could answer. "Jase, come quick."

Both he and Ryder appeared at Liam's side to see blood running down Gemma's face from her nose. Tears streaked down her cheeks, and she began crying in earnest.

"I don't feel good, Daddy." She held out her arms, and he took her gingerly, afraid he might hurt her, but she burrowed in close. Ryder came to him, and together they held her between the two of them, heedless of the blood staining their shirts. "Daddy." Her hiccupping sobs tore at his heart.

"What's going on?" His father placed his hand on Gemma's head to soothe her, while his mother called 911.

Everyone crowded around him, their anxious faces peering at Gemma, but only Gemma mattered at the moment. Ryder and Gemma.

"Ry, what's wrong? What do we do?" There'd never been a moment in his life where he'd been more terrified. Jason wanted to scream but had to remain calm for his daughter's sake.

Frightened blue eyes met his. "I don't know. Your mom already called the ambulance, so all we can do now is wait."

Gemma continued to cry into his chest, and helplessness overwhelmed him. At the sound of the sirens, relief flooded through him. Holding her close and with Ryder right by his side, Jason hurried to the front door, followed by the rest of his family.

"Daddy, I'm scared."

Her tiny voice stabbed him through the heart.

"Don't worry, baby. You're going to be fine. Everything will be okay."

Within minutes the paramedics had her on a stretcher in the back of the ambulance, and with him and Ryder holding her hands, they raced through the streets. He knew his parents would be right behind them.

GEMMA WAS WHISKED into pediatric emergency as soon as the ambulance pulled up outside the hospital. On the way, Ryder had let his own father know as well, but he was in Connecticut for the weekend. His parents, along with Liam and Mark, came running through the door to the emergency room waiting area a few minutes after their arrival.

"Jason, what's happening?" His mother's frightened eyes swam with tears. "Where is she?"

"Ryder is with her in the back. They're examining her now." When his mother hugged him, it was the first time Jason allowed himself to be afraid. "I'm so scared, Mom. What's happening? Everything was fine, and now all of a sudden—" His voice caught. "This never happened before."

His father put his arm around him. "You know how these kids pick up every germ on the playground."

But Jason heard the doubt in his father's voice, and his own fear remained. Gemma had always been so healthy; she'd sailed through the regular childhood maladies and mishaps with little problems. Unlike most children, she didn't cry when she went to the doctor for checkups and found the shots more annoying than painful.

Jason feared that this sudden onset of headaches, the unexplained bruising, and now the nosebleed were too out of character to be anything minor. And now that his family had arrived, he had to find Ryder and be with him and their little girl.

He approached the nurse's desk. "Hi, can I go back now to my husband and daughter?"

The harried nurse, who had the phone to her ear, tipped her head toward the swinging doors. "Room C."

Jason ran through the entrance to the emergency room, his eyes scanning the crowded pathway. Gurneys lined the aisles, people lying on them, groaning in pain, while police officers and EMT personnel stood at the nurses' station, filling out paperwork or congregating in small groups. So many people wore scrubs, Jason had no idea who was a nurse or a doctor.

He counted down the letters on the wall until he came to C and rushed toward the curtained-off room. When he drew back the drape, he saw Ryder's tense, white face fixated on Gemma; one hand held hers tight and the other rested on her head. Gemma seemed peaceful now, but her sweet face still seemed pale and her breathing somewhat shallow.

"Ry," he choked out. "I'm here."

Jason watched the relief settle in Ryder's eyes. He kissed Gemma's cheek and let go of her hand, but she didn't stir. Poor baby must be wiped out from fear and exhaustion. At least they were both with her and this didn't happen during the week while they were at work.

Ryder grabbed him; Jason could sense the fear in his trembling body as they hugged.

"Thank God you're here. She finally fell asleep." Jason watched the pain rise again in Ryder's eyes and knew it mirrored his own. "So many doctors have been in and out, but no one's told me a damn thing." Ryder raked his hand through his hair. "All I know is that they're running blood tests on her, but they won't have the results for a while."

They sat down next to Gemma's bed, hands clasped, their fingers laced together. Right from the start, they'd been each other's lifeline, and having had these magical years with their daughter, he refused to believe anything would take her away from them. He wished he could trade places with her and be in that bed.

"My dad said maybe it's one of those bugs the kids are always picking up. You know that happens all the time." The pleading in his voice did little to convince Ryder; Jason could see the doubt in his husband's beautiful blue eyes. Gemma had those same eyes.

"Yeah? I don't know. Somehow I think this is different, Jase." Ryder squeezed his hand. "All these things happening at once. She's only a baby."

"And we're going to have her until she grows into a beautiful woman; we'll be celebrating her Sweet Sixteen, high school graduation, and bringing her to college. I refuse to believe anything bad is going to happen to someone as innocent as Gemma."

The minutes ticked by as they sat by their daughter's side. Every once in a while a nurse or resident would pop their head in and peek at Gemma, but no one with answers or authority came to talk with them.

After they'd been there the better part of two hours, a doctor pulled open the drapes and walked inside. "Mr. Daniels, Mr. Mallory?" With a raised brow, he glanced at Gemma who had begun to stir from her sleep. "This is your daughter?"

"Yes." Jason dropped Ryder's hand and stood, towering over the slightly built, shorter man. "Gemma is ours. Now what can you tell us? What's wrong with her?"

Dr. Tanner, whose name Jason picked up from the tag on his chest, shook his head with regret. "We still aren't sure, and because of that we want to admit her."

"Daddy Jay?" Gemma's voice sounded so tiny and lost. "Where am I?"

"It's okay, baby. You're going to be fine. The nice doctors want to find out what happened, so you're going to stay here for a little while."

"No." Her eyes streamed tears, and she started to sob. "I wanna go home and see Nana." She began to hiccup and shake. "I want my doggies."

Ryder left his side to take her in his arms and try to soothe her pending hysteria, while Jason faced the doctor. "Are you keeping something from us we should know?"

"Not at all. We are running as many tests as we can with the blood sample we took at her arrival. Once we have more time, hopefully we'll have an answer for you." Dr. Tanner patted his arm awkwardly. "The orderlies will come and bring her upstairs. I'm sorry. I know there's nothing worse than a sick child."

Jason forgot about him as soon as he walked out, his concentration solely on his child. He and Ryder didn't leave her side for a minute—not when the orderlies came to take her upstairs to a room, or when they came to take more blood and she cried again.

His parents and brothers crowded into the room, making a big fuss over Gemma until she smiled a little. He and Ryder held on to each other, and Jason could almost feel the love flowing between them. Work, money, everything, faded to nothing. All that mattered was Ryder and Gemma. And if Ryder ever let him go, he'd fall apart.

Chapter Four

By Monday morning, after an entire weekend spent in the hospital, Ryder had almost forgotten what fresh air felt like. He and Jason stayed by Gemma's side at the hospital, only returning home twice to change their clothes. Normally they'd bring Pearl and Trouper to Jason's parents, but since they were also at the hospital that wasn't going to work. Naturally, Ryder had called on his best friends, Connor and Emily, to help, and like always, they were there for him.

"Of course we'll keep them." Emily's soft voice comforted him as it always had. "You know you don't have to think twice. Go be with Gemma, and when she gets out tell her she can help me take care of Isabel like a big sister."

"Thanks, Em. I don't know what we'd do without you and Connor. You're saving our lives here. Jason's parents are with us and—"

"Are you kidding me? You don't need to explain anything. You need us, we're there; simple as that," said Connor. "Go on to the hospital and don't worry about the dogs. We'll take them as long as necessary. But keep us in the loop. She's not only our goddaughter; Gemma's like our own child."

What would he ever do without these friends? "Thanks," he whispered, unwilling to trust his voice to utter more than one word. At any minute he might shatter to pieces, and he needed to make sure he showed up strong and positive for Gemma's sake. Four years had gone by so fast; it wasn't enough time.

Please. Don't take her away from us. He ended the conversation, and hearing Jason's footsteps in the hallway, Ryder wiped his eyes. Gemma would be fine, and they'd look back on this as a story to tell when she was grown up. How to scare the shit out of your parents.

"Ready, babe? I'm hoping the doctors will have some answers now that it's not the weekend." Ryder had talked to his father and filled him in on Gemma's symptoms. Like he knew he would, his father had already called in the best pediatric specialists in New York to come and give their opinion. Ryder had full faith in the doctors who had seen Gemma so far, but his father wouldn't hear of it. No one but the best for his granddaughter, as far as Alexander Daniels was concerned. "My dad and Denise are going to be there this morning too."

Jason came tripping around the corner, buttoning up his shirt. "Yeah, I'm ready, let's go." An overwhelming desire to hold Jason hit Ryder at that moment. He needed that connection between the two of them to face the day and whatever news they'd receive about their daughter.

"Hey, Jase?"

At his tone, Jason turned around. "Yeah?"

Ryder winced at the stark fear in Jason's eyes. "Come here." He held out his arms. Jason walked up to him, and Ryder hugged his solid strength close. "I need you for a moment. Before we face everyone, you know?"

Jason burrowed his face between Ryder's shoulder and neck, and Ryder held on to him tight. "When we fell in love, I never imagined anything could be better than hearing you tell me you loved me." He kissed Jason's wavy hair, loving his husband's familiar scent, drinking him in.

"Then we got married, and knowing you were mine forever made it that much better."

"I feel the same way, Ry. You're in my blood; I can't get enough of you."

He framed Jason's face in the palms of his hands. "Then Gemma was born, and this tiny child, a piece of us and the love we share, was like another layer of joy. I love you more than ever; you're not only my husband—you and Gemma are my life." Ryder blinked against the rush of tears. "If I lose her, I'm afraid of losing you, our life…our love."

Jason gripped him. "We aren't going to lose her. She has the best doctors, and they're going to tell us she's okay. Maybe she has a vitamin deficiency or something." Jason kissed him, hard and desperate. "You could never lose me; I can find you anywhere you are. Now let's go be with our daughter, and hopefully we can take her home."

"You're right. They're probably scaring us over nothing. I mean, she's never been sick a day in her life." With confidence building in his veins, Ryder followed Jason out the front door. For Gemma's sake they'd be strong and get her through whatever it was. He banked the emotions that still threatened and took Jason's hand.

The return trip to the hospital took little time, and Ryder couldn't help but smile when he and Jason walked into Gemma's room. All of Jason's family was there: Liam held a huge pink teddy bear in his lap, Mark and his girlfriend, Julie, sat at the foot of Gemma's bed, reading her a story, while Jessie, who came in from Vassar for the day, attempted to brush Gemma's hair.

"Oh, good, you're back." Helen, Jason's mother, hurried over to them, leaving Tony sitting next to the bed. "The nurse said the doctor will be here within half an hour."

"Daddy Ry, Daddy Jay, how are my doggies?" Gemma's lower lip wobbled. "I miss my Pearl and Trouper, and I bet they're sad 'cause I'm not home."

"Hi, sweetie-pie." Ryder leaned over to kiss her cheek. "Pearl and Trouper are at a play-date sleepover with Laurel and Hardy at Aunt Emily and Uncle Connor's house. Look, I'll show you a picture."

Her eyes brightened a bit when she took his phone

and stared at a picture of the four pit bulls with signs around their necks that spelled out *Get Well Gemma.* Emily had sent that to him just a few minutes ago—she always knew exactly the right thing to do.

"Oooh, I bet they're having fun." She lay back against the pillow. Jessie had finished brushing her hair and came around the bed to hug him, while Jason kissed Gemma and began to make funny faces with Liam to distract her.

"How are you really doing?" Her eyes searched his face. "I can't imagine how you and Jason are handling this." She rubbed his arm in comfort.

With family, there was no need to fake or hide his emotions, and Ryder had never been well versed in lying. "I'm terrible—scared and nervous, yet we have to keep up this happy pretense for Gem's sake."

"I'll bet." She glanced over at Gemma, then back to him. "Poor thing. Do you have any idea what it is?"

Ryder shook his head. "Not a clue. Jason thinks maybe a vitamin deficiency, but he's only talking out of thin air."

Gemma began to pluck at the bedcovers with restless fingers. "I wanna go home. When can I go home?"

"Soon, baby, soon. The doctor will be here, and then we'll know everything."

Ryder's father and his wife, Denise, walked in with another big teddy bear. Gemma's eyes lit up. "Grandpa. Grandma." She held out her arms.

From the moment he'd seen Gemma as a newborn,

Alexander Daniels, one of New York City's most feared corporate lawyers, had been unable to resist her. Ryder still marveled at how his staid and conservative father turned to mush whenever Gemma merely smiled at him. Though Ryder and his brother hadn't had much of a relationship with their father growing up, the three had grown close since he and Jason had married.

"How's my baby girl?"

"Grandpa, I tole you, I'm not a baby. I want Grandma."

"That's right, Alex, Gemma is a big girl. That's why she gets the biggest teddy bears, right?" Denise smiled and hugged Gemma.

Ryder's throat closed, making it hard to swallow. When his father had filed for divorce, his mother hadn't contested it, and he deserved to be in a relationship with a person who loved him. Denise gave his father all the love and attention he never saw between his parents. In all their years of marriage Ryder couldn't recall ever seeing them physically touch. He wondered if his mother had ever loved his father, and if not, why she'd married him. His neck ached, and he rubbed it, his troubled thoughts spinning through his mind.

And despite everything, Ryder still couldn't help wish his mother would one day magically turn around, ask for forgiveness, and try and forge a relationship with him and his family. How could she not want to see her own granddaughter? The greatest joy in their lives, Jason's parents repeated every weekend, was watching their children grow their families. Ryder knew the Sundays they spent at Helen and Tony's with all of Jason's family, and sometimes his own father and brother, were the best times of their lives. The memories created were irreplaceable, and they cherished the pictures from every get-together.

For the next half hour, they all did everything they could to keep Gemma distracted: played games with her, told her funny stories, Jessie and Denise braided her hair in an elaborate style. Feathery wisps of hair curled around her face, and it was all Ryder could do to keep from gathering her in his arms and running away with her. The fierce urge to protect her beat hot within his blood, and he vowed nothing would hurt her as long as he lived. Whatever he had to do for his child, he would.

"Ryder Daniels, Jason Mallory?" A woman in a white coat stood at the door.

Ryder and Jason jumped up and strode over to her. "I'm Ryder, and this is my husband, Jason." He took Jason's hand in his; Jason's damp palm trembled, and he squeezed it.

"I'm Dr. Fleischer, the hematologist. I've been working on your daughter's case."

Ryder's heart bounced in his chest and sweat broke over his body. "Case? Why does she need a case? What's wrong?"

Dr. Fleischer gave him a sympathetic smile. "Let's go outside and talk, shall we?" Without waiting for an answer, she walked out, leaving Jason and him to scramble after her. She led them to a private office, closed the door behind them after they entered, and didn't speak until they were seated. Ryder sat at the edge of the straight-backed wooden chair, his hand clasping Jason's. He'd never been this scared in his life.

"Doctor, please. What's going on? Gemma's never been sick; she's always been the healthiest girl since she was a baby. We take her to the pediatrician regularly and she's up-to-date on all her shots." Ryder knew he should shut up and listen to what the doctor had to say, but he felt like they were on trial and needed to defend himself and Jason and their parenting.

"I can see that from her records. She's a lovely little girl; you both must be very proud." The encouraging smile the doctor gave them relaxed Ryder for a moment.

"We are." He glanced over at Jason, who gave him a brief smile and squeezed his hand. "She means everything to us."

The doctor's smile faded. "Gemma is going to need all the love and support you and your family can give her in the coming months."

"Why?" Jason demanded. "What's wrong?"

Nausea rose in Ryder's throat, and he began to shake. How naive of them to believe life would allow them uncomplicated joy. He'd always known something would come along to shatter the perfect world they'd created. Ryder swallowed hard, forcing himself to concentrate on the doctor's voice.

The doctor leaned over the desk and crossed her

arms over the files that rested on top.

"Your daughter has aplastic anemia, a severe case. It explains the sudden onset of headaches, bruising, and nosebleeds. They are all classic symptoms of this disease."

"Disease? Gemma?" The room whirled, and Ryder thought he might pass out. He had to drop his head into his hands and take deep breaths to keep himself from fainting. After taking a few steadying breaths, he raised his head and leaned against a shaking Jason. "I don't understand. What is this anemia? Some sort of blood disease?"

"Yes." The doctor gave both him and Jason handouts, but Ryder couldn't read anything. All the words ran together, and he couldn't concentrate. Nothing seemed real; only the feel of Jason's arm around him kept him from falling apart.

"Quite often this disease is caused by prolonged exposure to certain drugs or chemicals. We know that isn't the case here. Unfortunately, many people, children included, get aplastic anemia, and we never know the cause of its onset. But Gemma definitely has it, and we have to plan the course of treatment."

Scrubbing his face with his hands, Ryder attempted to see things with a clear head. He liked this doctor; she spoke kindly and was no-nonsense. "But it can be treated, right? Like with a blood transfusion or medicine?"

"Poor Gemma, she hates taking even a vitamin."

Jason grimaced. "She is not going to be happy about this."

Ryder gazed expectantly at the doctor, waiting for her to rattle off the treatment. Instead, dread curled through him at the shadows in her eyes. "It's not going to be that simple, is it, Dr. Fleischer?" His voice cracked. "What's going on? Tell us."

THOUGH THE DOCTOR spoke plainly and in a calm, measured tone, Jason had trouble wrapping his head around the words that came out of her mouth. She might have been talking gibberish or backward for all the sense she made.

"Please. I'm sorry if I sound stupid, but I don't understand. She's sick? Like really sick? Isn't there some kind of medicine she can take, or I always heard about taking more iron if your blood isn't healthy." Jason's own head hurt now, and he ran his hands through his hair. "She hates spinach, but I'm sure if we told her she had to eat it, she would."

The doctor came from behind her desk to sit with them. No encouraging smile lit her eyes or lightened her face. "Ryder, Jason, I'm afraid it's much more serious than that. If it were only a matter of a change in diet or a pill, we wouldn't be having this conversation."

"Then what is it?" Jason whispered. Ryder shifted closer and took his hand once again.

"Your daughter is a very sick little girl. From the

severity of the anemia, it's my opinion she needs a bone-marrow transplant as soon as possible."

"What?" Ryder cried out. "Bone-marrow transplant? Does she have cancer?"

"No, but for this type of disease, a bone-marrow transplant is the best and quickest way to save her life."

Save her life? Disease? Our baby?

This couldn't be happening. Jason thought he might be sick. His stomach churned and he couldn't catch his breath. Someone pressed a bottle of water into his hand, and he wrenched it open, then drank half of it down. Shuddering, he managed to draw two deep breaths before he could focus.

Gazing at Ryder's anguished face, the tears Jason had held back broke through. They clung together for a moment, drawing strength from each other. In their years together, Ryder had always been Jason's rock, and he needed Ryder's strength more than ever now.

After a minute, he and Ryder separated. The doctor handed them tissues, and Jason wiped his eyes but didn't throw his away. He had a feeling he'd need plenty of them before the day was through.

"I know it's a very scary thing to hear, but we have every confidence if we find a suitable donor and do the transplant, Gemma can recover to live a full and normal life."

Those words did little to ease the pain in Jason's chest, and from Ryder's devastated expression, he felt the same way.

"If? What do you mean if? I'm sure one of us will be able to donate to her. We're her family."

"Jase, let the doctor tell us. What happens next?" Jason knew Ryder, always the practical one, would need all his questions answered. "What do we need to do to help Gemma?"

Dr. Fleischer consulted her clipboard. "We'll need to hospitalize Gemma and begin radiation to clean out her bone marrow. While that is happening, all relatives will need to be tested to see if they are capable of being a bone-marrow donor." She glanced up from the papers. "I presume you used a surrogate, or was Gemma adopted?"

Jason couldn't speak; radiation, bone-marrow transplants—he couldn't begin to understand any of this. She was only a little girl. Mute, he stared over at Ryder, who paid no attention to him but rather, sat in concentrated thought. A least one of them would be able to deal with this because Jason teetered on the edge of a breakdown.

"We used a surrogate, and both our sperm was utilized for the fertilization process. When Gem was two we did a DNA test, and it determined I was her natural father, and Jason formally adopted her." Ryder slipped his arms around Jason's neck. "She's both of ours, by blood and love."

A broad smile crossed Dr. Fleischer's face. "That's lovely. Are you in contact with the mother? Are there any siblings?"

Shaking himself into action, Jason pulled out his

phone to look up Shannon's telephone number. His child needed him, and he couldn't sit by doing nothing. "Yes, she lives in the city with her husband. I'll text her now." It took only a moment for him to text her to contact them as soon as possible.

"We have to tell the family," said Ryder, his face creased with pain. "This is going to kill your parents, my father." He groaned. "Christ, what a mess."

"Give me everyone's name, and we can send them today to be tested to see if they're a match. It's a simple swab, no needles." Dr. Fleischer pulled out a pen and flipped her notebook open.

Ryder listed everyone in the hospital room, plus Landon and Nicole. They hadn't said anything to either of them; Landon was on Law Review at Columbia Law School working his ass off, and Nicole was in Boston. They hadn't ever imagined it would be necessary.

"What about the baby?" Jason explained his brother and sister-in-law had recently had a son. "You can't take marrow from him; he's too tiny."

"Agreed," said Dr. Fleischer. "We'll work through all the adults on the list first." She checked all the names and familial connections. "Ryder, your mother isn't listed. Is she still living?"

Debatable. Jason waited to hear what Ryder would say.

"We haven't spoken in years; she doesn't accept my life or Jason as my husband."

The smile on Dr. Fleischer's face dimmed. "She's

never met her granddaughter?"

"No." Ryder huddled in his chair, and as always whenever Ryder's mother came up in conversation, Jason put his arm around Ryder, letting him know he was loved, no matter how hatefully his mother behaved toward him. "We haven't spoken since before Jason and I got married."

"Forget about her, Ry." Jason hugged him close and kissed his cheek. "We don't need her; we never have. We've come this far without her, and we'll make it all the way without."

"I'm afraid it's not that simple, Jason." Dr. Fleischer circled the desk and sat behind it. She leaned her chin on her fist. "Ryder's mother is a potential donor for Gemma because Gemma shares her DNA."

"But that means Ry should be an even better match," said Jason stubbornly. "He's closer to Gemma than his mother."

"Jase." Ryder covered his hand with his own palm. "I don't think we need to discuss this in front of the doctor."

"Unfortunately, it doesn't always work that way. Sometimes a close relative's bone marrow isn't an exact match while a stranger's might be. It's the reason we need to have everyone tested." The doctor shot him a troubled look. "My office will set up appointments to have you all come in for testing. We get the results in three to five days."

Right now, all Jason wanted was to be with his little

girl, his husband, and his family. "We'll all get tested, and I'm sure you'll find a donor among us." Still holding Ryder's hand, he stood. "You'll let us know what we have to do, right? I want to get back to Gemma and prepare her for staying in the hospital and not seeing her friends and her dogs."

"Of course, I understand." She shook both of their hands. "Please know that once we do the transplant, we're hopeful for a full recovery for your little girl."

Jason gave her a tight smile. "Thank you."

Ryder thanked her, and they hurried out down the hallway, back to Gemma's room. Before they reached the doorway, Jason hesitated and held Ryder back.

"After we all talk to Gemma, I'll call Shannon and explain what happened if I still haven't heard from her."

"I hope she's still around; we agreed to minimal contact after Gemma's birth." Ryder frowned. "Who knows if she even lives in the city anymore?"

"Fuck it, Ry, stop being so negative." But Jason was also concerned; he hadn't yet received an answering text back from Shannon.

"I'm not being negative; I'm being realistic. If none of us are able to be donors, we'll need to reach her and my mother."

"Let's see what happens." He kissed Ryder, and they held each other tight. "All that matters is for us to be together and for Gemma to know we're here for her no matter what."

Ryder gave him a strange look. "Why would that

even be an issue? I love you, and that's never going to change." He tugged Jason's hand. "Let's go in and talk to everyone."

Jason followed but couldn't rid himself of the nagging dread that his entire life was about to explode.

Chapter Five

LIFE REVOLVED AROUND the hospital for him and Jason. It had been over a week since Gemma had been admitted, and both their families had undergone bone-marrow testing to see if they were a match. At each phone call or text Ryder's heart jumped, dreading and yet hoping at the same time it would be the call from the hospital notifying him that they'd found a match.

All of Jason's family had already been notified earlier in the week that they weren't suitable matches, Jason included. Ryder grimaced, remembering that painful phone call. Jason had turned pale and refused to talk for the rest of the day until he broke down.

"I thought maybe I'd be able to help her, that by some chance I'd be a match. Now I'm nothing."

"Oh, babe, you help her by being her daddy, by loving her and always being there for her. And you aren't nothing. You're everything to us." Ryder had spent that night holding Jason, loving him so fiercely and completely that Jason could barely move in the morning.

His phone rang, and his pulse quickened, but when

he checked the number, it was his father.

"Hi, Dad."

"Ryder. I got a call from the hospital. I'm not a match, nor is Denise." For the first time in his life, Ryder listened to his father cry. "I hoped I could help her. I'd give my life for her, you know that, right?"

"Of course I do, we all feel the same way." Ryder lay on the sofa, Pearl at his side. Jason had gone out for a run with Trouper. He scratched Pearl's ears, and she thumped her tail. "Jason's a wreck, and I'm still waiting to hear. Maybe that's a good sign, huh?"

Ryder turned on the sofa to hug Pearl. Even when he was alone or had that fight with Jason before they got together, he'd never felt such utter hopelessness and despair.

"I'm praying every day. Denise and I both are. Have you been there today?"

"Yeah. We had breakfast with her this morning; then Helen and Tony came to spend the afternoon with her. Connor and Emily will be by later when they can get a sitter for the kids. Jason and I will go back after we get a quick bite. We were there all night with her." Thank God they had such a devoted circle of family and friends; since she'd been admitted, Gemma hadn't been alone.

"Good. We'll also be there tonight; Denise promised to watch a movie with her."

Despite his heavy heart, Ryder smiled. "I bet they've seen it a hundred times already."

"Denise would watch it a million times for Gemma."

The door opened, and Trouper bounded in, Jason trailing behind him, holding a pizza box. Ryder gave him the thumbs-up sign. It might've been their second pizza of the week or their third. It didn't matter. All food tasted like sawdust to him anyway.

"I have to go, Dad. Jason just walked in with lunch. I'll see you tonight."

He ended the call, and while Jason set the pizza box on the table, Ryder got out the plates and took two bottles of beer from the refrigerator then joined him, sliding him one of the bottles, while keeping the other in front of himself.

"He's not a match, nor is Denise. So that leaves me as the last resort." Ryder opened the box and put one of the crisp wedges onto a plate. He handed it to Jason. "I'm not feeling too hopeful."

"I am." Jason took the pizza slice and wandered back into the living room. He slumped onto the sofa and put his feet up on the coffee table. "You're her biological father; her real father; you're bound to be the best match."

In two quick strides, Ryder joined Jason on the sofa. "Stop saying that. You're her real father as much as I am. We discussed this when we first decided to use a surrogate." Ryder took the plate with the pizza from Jason and put it on the table. "You don't honestly think that?"

Jason shrugged and failed to meet his eyes. "I dunno, maybe."

"Oh, babe." Ryder cupped Jason's cheek and kissed his lips, and as always, the taste and scent of his husband set off a wild hunger Ryder found himself hard-pressed to control. "You're not only the best father to Gemma, you're the best husband," Ryder kissed Jason, plunging his tongue into Jason's mouth, swirling and tangling it with Jason's tongue before burying his face in Jason's neck. "My best friend."

They remained on the sofa kissing, needing to reconnect after days and nights spent at the hospital, worrying over Gemma. Ryder hadn't realized how much he missed Jason's touch, his smell, and taste. With his husband spread out beneath him, Ryder knew it was time to take care of Jason.

"Let's go to the bedroom." He stood, his body throbbing with need, and held out a hand to Jason. "We haven't spent any time together in almost a week, and I want you."

"Want you too." Jason jumped up, and with their arms around each other, they walked toward their bedroom, stopping to kiss every few steps.

Ryder's neglected libido flamed back to life. He stripped his clothes off and flung them across the room, his avid gaze never leaving Jason as he watched him shuck his shorts, T-shirt, and boxers. His muscled chest, covered with swirls of dark, silky hair, proved too much of a temptation, and Ryder stepped close, sliding his hands across the hard dips and planes of Jason's torso.

"Jase," Ryder whispered, unable to control the urgency now building within him. "I need you so much right now." Chest to chest, they stood pressed together, hearts beating in sync.

Jason drew back the covers and lay down on the bed. Ryder joined him, their erections brushing, providing tantalizing friction, but not enough to satisfy Ryder, who needed Jason inside him to be complete and whole again after the numbing horror of the past week.

Capturing Jason's mouth with his own, Ryder tried to convey his desire, his hands roaming over Jason's body, smoothing over hot skin and hard muscle.

"Jase, please." Ryder dug his hands into the meat of Jason's shoulders and thrust his hips forward. Pleasure-pain rocketed through Ryder at the touch of Jason's hand on his cock, and he moaned, the sound echoing off the bedroom walls.

"Oh God, yeah, there."

When Jason moved and stopped touching him Ryder almost whined in frustration, but within a moment, Jason was back, a small bottle of lube in his hand. At the touch of Jason's now-cool, slick fingers, Ryder sighed, lay on his back, and opened himself up wide to his husband.

"Fuck me, now." There was nothing pretty or romantic between them, their almost desperate coupling a way back to each other, and as Jason prepped him, Ryder welcomed the harshness of Jason's touch, craving the sting and burn of being stretched.

"Babe, hurry, please," he urged, and held his arms out to gather Jason close. Jason complied, and the moment Ryder felt the head of Jason's cock at his entrance, he pushed down, taking him inside, loving the hard penetration. Only Jason had ever been able to provide him the emotional connection to the physical act of love, and as they rocked together, Ryder accepting Jason's deep thrusts, his fractured world settled back into place.

"Yes," Ryder gasped, and stars exploded behind his eyes. "Jase, Jase," he sobbed, and knew it wouldn't be much longer before he came, his own cock hard and aching. He reached down to give himself a few hard tugs, and then he was there, spurting hot across his stomach and chest, his balls mashed up against Jason every time he plunged into Ryder's body.

Shattered and sated Ryder knew, with the familiarity born of living with Jason, exactly when Jason headed to that point of no return. His head arched up, accentuating the strong muscles of his neck and shoulders, and his drive within Ryder's body strengthened.

"Ry," gasped Jason, and Ryder felt it then, the hot wet heat inside him as Jason came. Ryder held Jason close, waiting for him to stop shaking, murmuring loving words into Jason's ear. They lay together, and for a moment all was right with their world, the frightening uncertainty of Gemma's illness held in abeyance almost like a dream.

Jason pulled out slowly and went into the bathroom, and Ryder instantly missed the security his heavy warmth always provided. He needn't have worried though, for Jason returned only minutes later. No words were necessary; by mutual understanding he and Jason remained in bed, perhaps drawing comfort and strength from each other to make it through the rest of the day and night. Jason wiped him up with a damp washcloth he brought back, and they lay together, catching their breaths and holding each other.

Then Ryder heard it, the faint but unmistakable ring of his cell phone.

"Shit, I'd better get it. It could be the hospital calling." Naked, he scrambled out of bed, leaving Jason behind. Remembering he'd left it on the sofa downstairs, he ran there first and was rewarded by the sight of its flashing screen.

"Hello?" He flopped down on the sofa, ignoring his nakedness, the stickiness of his body and the two dogs crowding around him for attention. "Hello?"

"Hello, Ryder? It's Dr. Fleischer."

"Is everything okay? Did something happen to Gemma?"

"No, Gemma is fine. She received another transfusion today and is resting comfortably. I stopped in to check on her a little while ago, and Jason's parents are there."

"Good, all right."

"The reason I'm calling is we received the result of

your bone-marrow test, and I'm afraid you aren't a match."

"What?" His voice rang so loud Pearl whined, and he shushed her but put his arm around her thick neck. She'd been there through every major event in his life, and he needed her solid reality next to him. "That can't be. I'm her father, her blood father. How is this possible?"

Dr. Fleischer's sympathetic voice spoke in that calm, precise way he'd already grown accustomed to. "The same way her mother, Shannon, also isn't a match. Sometimes it works like that. We've reached the point, however, where we've entered Gemma into the National Match Foundation, for her to be matched up with a bone-marrow volunteer." She paused. "I urge you to contact your mother. She might be a match, Ryder, and Gemma should have that chance."

In a daze, he thanked the doctor and hung up. Unable to stand and return to Jason in the bedroom, Ryder remained on the sofa with the dogs, who with their innate sense of understanding people's moods, stayed close by him, licking his hands and face.

"Ry, what's the matter? Who was that?" Jason knelt by his side. His silky hair lay in messy waves, and his dark blue eyes glowed with contentment.

An impending sense of loss struck Ryder, and he grabbed on to Jason, pulling him close. "That was the doctor." He spoke into the curve of Jason's neck, inhaling his heady scent. "I'm not a match either, Jase.

Now none of us are." Tears pricked behind his lashes.

"Fuck." Jason squeezed him close. "I can't fucking believe this."

There was little left to say. They trudged back upstairs to shower and dress, neither of them speaking a word. Depressed and broken, Ryder headed into the kitchen to reheat the pizza. He did it by rote, without thinking. Ryder took the pizza out of the oven and slid the crispy slices onto the plates Jason had given him, and Jason opened the two beers Ryder had taken out earlier and twisted their caps off, setting them next to each plate on the kitchen table. Normally Gemma sat between them, and her booster seat remained as a glaring reminder of how much they had to lose. Ryder braced his hands on the table, allowing the tears to come.

"Why her? It's not right. She's too little to understand. It should've been me."

"God, Ry." Jason grabbed him, pulling him tight against his chest. "Don't say that. It shouldn't happen to anyone. I don't know why this happened, but we have to stay strong for her."

Ashamed at his outburst, Ryder took a deep breath and then exhaled into Jason's neck. "I know. I feel so helpless and frustrated."

"I know, babe. We all are." Jason kissed his cheek. "It's hitting home right now that nothing is in our hands anymore when it comes to our daughter, and it scares me too. We're her parents, and yet we can't protect or help her."

Jason put their unspoken fears into words. For the first time since she was born, they had no control over their child. No matter how much they loved Gemma, it wasn't enough. And now their one hope rested with a person who refused to acknowledge he existed, and Ryder had doubts about whether he could persuade his mother to not only see him but help his daughter. How could she refuse an innocent child? Even she wasn't so cruel.

Was she?

They separated and sat down to eat. Ryder took one bite, but the normally delicious pizza tasted as appetizing as a raw potato, and he tossed the slice back on the plate. He glanced over to see Jason staring at Gemma's empty seat, and Ryder's resolve strengthened. If he had to break into his mother's apartment and tie her to a chair, he would make her listen to him.

"When we get home from the hospital tonight I'm going to call my mother."

Screwing up his face as if he bit into a lemon, Jason curled his lips. He opened his mouth, but Ryder cut him off.

"I know what you're going to say. You don't want me to. But we have no choice."

Jason fiddled with the neck of the beer bottle, peeling away the paper label. "I know we don't, and that's what's driving me crazy. That after everything she did to you and your brother and how she's even refused to acknowledge our marriage and daughter, we have to go to her to ask for a favor." He smacked the table with his hand. "It pisses me off to have to crawl to her."

"But, Jase," said Ryder, keeping his voice reasonable when his mother's behavior was anything but. "What are we supposed to do? She's Gemma's blood grandmother whether we like it or not. We have to give our daughter every chance for life."

"Of course we do. But I want to be there with you. You shouldn't have to go alone. We'll face her together and show her what a strong family we are."

Surprised, Ryder picked up his slice again and took a bite, not so much because he was hungry, but to choose his words carefully so as not to upset Jason. He chewed and swallowed, then set the slice down.

"This isn't the time to convince her to accept us as a family or even me as her son. At this point my only concern is getting her to agree to testing."

Instead of answering him, Jason gazed down at his half-eaten slice, the silence thickening until it sat like an ominous force between them.

"What, you don't agree?" No longer hungry, Ryder crumpled his plate and threw it, along with the pizza, into the garbage pail. Facing Jason again, Ryder nudged him with his foot. "Answer me. What's going on in your mind?"

"I never imagined you'd do it on your own. We're her parents, both of us. And both of us should be there."

He hitched his chair closer to Jason's. "And under

normal circumstances, I'd completely agree. This is anything but. To inject more strife and controversy when we need her in a life-or-death situation is drawing away the focus from the importance of the visit. I need to do this alone."

Deep lines not visible a few weeks ago now etched grooves across Jason's forehead. "I don't have to like it, but I see your point."

"You're adorable when you grumble."

"I'm sorry, Ry. I didn't mean to bully you. I've never been so helpless in my life."

Not knowing any other way to comfort Jason, Ryder kissed him, feeling the same way, more determined than ever to see his mother, no matter what it took.

Chapter Six

JASON BARELY SPOKE with Ryder during their trip to the hospital. It wasn't so much that he was upset about Ryder contacting his mother; rationally he knew she needed to be tested. Anything to save Gemma's life needed to be done as soon as possible. But Ryder doing it all on his own, instead of bringing Jason along as his husband and Gemma's father, bothered him more than he wanted to admit. Before Gemma's diagnosis, he'd felt like they were slipping away from each other with his heavy work schedule, and now with Ryder handling his mother on his own, Jason felt completely lost.

But nothing—not a disagreement with Ryder, nor his own nagging fears over their lives being manipulated by forces beyond their control—nothing would intrude upon his time with Gemma. Before he entered her room, Jason made sure he put on a brave face, and his heart swelled with love at the sight of all his family crowded around Gemma's bed. Stuffed animals, balloons, and pictures of Pearl and Trouper filled the room. Connor and Emily had taken the dogs the day before, and from the hospital he, Ryder, and Gemma video-chatted with them so Gemma could talk to her doggies. Jason didn't know who was more excited, Gemma or the pups. Afterward, though, she had cried in his arms, begging to come home. Jason had no idea where he and Ryder would find the strength to tell her that not only couldn't she go home, but also about all the medical procedures coming her way. How could she be expected to understand what was happening, when neither he nor Ryder did?

But not now. Today he planned on spending as much time as possible with his little girl, reading her favorite stories and doing whatever he could. Guilt still ate away at his insides at how much he'd missed over the past few months by working such late hours, and he vowed that if, no, *when* Gemma came back home, healthy again, he wouldn't let the business suck the life out of him. He hoped he got the chance.

"Hi, sweetie." Jason went to Gemma's bedside and sat down next to her, noting her pale skin and the shadows beneath her eyes. It killed him to see her like this. There was little left of the dancing girl of only a week ago. Tears threatened, and Jason inhaled deeply, willing them away. He'd never cried so much in all his life.

"Daddy Jay." She hugged him and whispered in his ear. "I wanna go home with you and Daddy Ry tonight. Can't I, please?"

Jason heard the slight hitch in her voice, and it almost brought him to his knees. No child should have to go through this. "We have to get you better first. Then you and I are gonna snuggle together with all your stuffed animals and have as many tea parties as you want."

"We don't do tea parties; we play pirates."

"Aye aye, Captain." He pretend-saluted her.

At the touch of a hand on his back he stiffened, only to relax at the sound of his mother's voice.

"Jason, Gemma's been such a good girl today."

He turned to his mother and forced a smile to his lips. "I'm sure she has. She's always been the best girl." He scanned the room and found Ryder talking to his father and Landon. He couldn't hear what Ryder said, but Jason knew. From the angry grimace on Landon's face to the air of tired resignation in Alexander Daniels' eyes, Jason understood how difficult this was for Ryder, yet watching the discussion unfold with his father and brother and not being a part of it stabbed him in the heart.

Gemma took his phone, and he put on the video of Pearl and Trouper playing in the park with Laurel and Hardy for her to watch. He took his mother's hand and led her over to where his father sat, on the opposite side of the room from Ryder.

"Ryder got the news today he's not a match either." The devastation on their faces matched his own. "There's no one left to test," he said, his gaze flickering over to Ryder, "except—"

"His mother, right?" Helen Mallory pursed her lips in anger.

"Yeah." Jason stretched out in the chair next to his father. "The thought of having to go to that woman for anything burns me."

Tony patted his arm. "That's gotta be hard on Ryder, knowing he has to talk to her after so long."

"Maybe he shouldn't."

Both his parents stared at him. "What are you talking about? She needs to be tested to see if she's a donor."

"Of course she does, I know that, but maybe Ryder shouldn't be the one to ask her. Let Landon or his father do it, or have the doctor call. She's never acknowledged us or Gemma. Why should he go crawling to her?"

His mother put her arms around him. "Oh, honey, I know it's hard, but Ryder is doing what he thinks is best."

Miserable and lonelier than he'd ever felt in his life, Jason watched Ryder stare out the window, his face as remote and untouchable as the stars. For the first time in years, Jason felt disconnected from Ryder, and he trembled, unsure and adrift. Alexander and Landon stood huddled in the corner talking quietly, but Jason could only concentrate on how unhappy and distant Ryder looked.

"He doesn't want me to be there. He thinks I'll be a distraction."

"He's right."

His father's response startled him.

"Let me ask you something." His mother put a hand on his arm, forcing his attention away from Ryder. "Why does it matter so much to you how his mother gets asked, as long as she comes around and gets tested? That's the real goal."

"Of course it is. Don't you think I know that? She's my daughter. I'll do anything for her. I only wanted to be there to support him because I know how hard it's going to be for him to have to see her now. But Ryder disagreed and told me he could handle it himself. He didn't even want to hear my opinion. This is our daughter, and I thought he'd at least listen to what I had to say."

"I'm sure it isn't easy for Ryder to think about talking to his mother, especially after everything that's happened between the two of them. But as we all know, this isn't about you, or Ryder, or Ryder's mother. It's not about any of us." His mother wiped away the tears slipping down her face. "It's about my baby in that bed and getting her well as quickly as possible. She's the only one who matters here. I'd give my life for her; we all would. So let Ryder do what he has to do, and you be there for him to support him and stay by his side."

Often you need someone a step outside your circle to bring some clarity. "Don't cry, Mom. You're right. I'm being an idiot. I'm so damn scared and frustrated I'm not thinking straight."

"Give Ryder your love. That's what he needs right now."

What a blessing to have parents like his. No matter that his father at first didn't understand his feelings for Ryder, or that he and his brother Liam had almost come to blows. Because of their mutual respect and love, they worked through the initial resistance to his and Ryder's relationship, and Jason knew his family unequivocally not only accepted Ryder but loved him and adored Gemma.

He'd make certain to show that same support to Ryder. He never imagined he'd find someone to love who would become so absolutely necessary to his life. Ryder was more than a husband or a partner; he was a part of Jason, his breath, his sweat, and now the tears they shared over their baby. Jason vowed to stand by him and be there, however Ryder needed him, to help him talk to his mother.

Together, forever. The two of them.

"I'll tell him tonight when we get home. I won't let him think he's going to go through this alone. That even if I'm not at his side physically, I'm there with him."

"Good, sweetheart. Imagine how he must feel, having to face her by himself. The last thing he needs on his mind is the burden of thinking you're upset or angry with him, when his focus has to be on making that woman understand she must do this. There is no choice for her. I know how persuasive Ryder can be, but with an opponent as coldly cruel as you've said his mother is, he needs to be better than good. This is the biggest trial of his life, and his focus has to be on figuring out how to talk to her."

From the moment he and Ryder met, their concentration had been solely on each other. And though Ryder's love had brought Jason such unexpected happiness, Gemma's birth elevated their relationship, bringing him not only joy but the realization that her very life rested in his hands. That sobering thought terrified him. It dawned on him now, the terrible burden on Ryder's shoulders and how selfish he'd been to add to its weight.

Throughout the entire evening, Jason made several attempts to pull Ryder aside to speak with him, but whether Ryder deliberately ignored him or honestly was too centered on Gemma, Jason didn't know. They didn't have a chance to talk freely until they were riding home in the cab.

"Hey, Ry?" Jason put his hand on Ryder's thigh, which pressed up against his own.

"Hmm?" Ryder continued to stare out the window, not turning to look at him or take his hand.

"I was wrong. I'm sorry I was such a dick."

A hint of a smile played around Ryder's lips. "Yeah, you were." Finally he put his hand over Jason's. "And I mean about both things. You were wrong, and you were being a dick."

"No need to rub it in," Jason muttered, but he turned his palm up and squeezed Ryder's hand.

The cab pulled up in front of their house. When he

and Ryder married, they decided it wasn't fair for Pearl and Trouper to live in Ryder's apartment in the city, so Ryder had moved to Jason's house in Brooklyn. It worked out perfectly, as the house was close enough for Jason's parents to stop by during the day and take the dogs out or bring them over to their own house where they could play in the fenced backyard, under Tony's watchful eye.

Ryder paid the cabdriver, and they walked up the steps and onto the front porch. Jason loved their house with the red-brick porch. In the summer flower pots of geraniums sat on the stoop. With a pang, he prayed Gemma would be here next summer to play in the garden and plant the sunflowers she loved so much.

"I've got something else that needs rubbing, as a matter of fact." Ryder leaned over and kissed him, and Jason pressed up hard against Ryder's chest, hungry to have Ryder beneath him, naked and calling out his name.

"Last one in the bedroom naked has to clean up the dog poop after we pick up Pearl and Trouper."

The door banged in his face as Ryder took off, shedding his clothes as he ran, and Jason's heart beat lighter than it had all day as he followed, admiring his husband's body. He unbuttoned his shirt and stood at the bedroom doorway while Ryder lay on the bed, stroking his erection.

"I win." For the first time in days, Ryder's grin reached his eyes. Jason tore off the rest of his clothes and joined him on the bed, kissing his way down Ryder's chest. He engulfed Ryder's cock in his mouth, taking him deep into the back of his throat. Jason knew Ryder's special spots, the ultrasensitive places to drive him wild, and he employed every teasing trick until Ryder lay writhing beneath him, his eyes heavy-lidded and glazed with desire.

"Fuck, Jase, I can't hold back."

Jason, his mouth full of Ryder, answered by drawing harder on Ryder's cock and grazing along the shaft with his teeth. Ryder cried out and bucked wildly, his hands clutching and twisting in the sheets.

"Oh, fuck."

Ryder climaxed hot and hard down Jason's throat, and Jason held him firm, taking every last drop until Ryder softened and slid out of his mouth. Jason sat back on his heels, surveying his husband's limp body glistening with sweat. The bed was in complete disarray, with the pillows tossed on the floor and the sheets half ripped from the mattress. Ryder lay splayed out in the center, his chest heaving, a smile on his face, looking totally spent. Jason's cock swelled, and he stroked it, his body vibrating to be inside Ryder.

Without opening his eyes, Ryder smiled. "What are you waiting for, an invitation? Get over here."

Jason didn't hesitate a second before he pounced on Ryder, kissing him feverishly. His familiar taste and scent, the feel of smooth, hard muscles under his skin set off a fire in Jason's belly that roared through him unchecked.

"God, I miss you."

"Miss you too, babe."

"I'm sorry I was a jerk."

"Mmm, s'okay." Ryder nipped and sucked at his neck. "Make it up to me now."

Jason scooted over to the night table to get the lube and slicked himself up while watching Ryder. He joined him back in the center of their king-sized bed and spread Ryder's legs open, kissing the inside of his thighs, nibbling up to the slant of his hip bone, all the while his slick fingers played havoc with Ryder's hole, slipping in and out to tease him.

Ryder's needy, desperate gasps echoed in the silent room, his hands scrabbling at the bedsheets while his head thrashed side to side.

"Fuck. Me."

"Yeah." Jason guided himself inside, feeling the wondrously tight heat engulf him. "How's that?"

"Perfect." Ryder folded his legs to his chest, and Jason sank in deeper, as deep as he could until his balls lay up against Ryder's ass and his forehead touched Ryder's. "You're perfect."

Without speaking, Jason rocked back and forth into Ryder, sliding in and out of the body he knew as well as his own by now, yet as always, making love to Ryder never got old or stale, each touch a fresh awakening, every kiss and caress unfurling a passion only the two of them created together.

Too soon, too fast, his climax rolled over him, and Jason shivered and trembled, attempting unsuccessfully to forestall the end of their lovemaking. He wanted to stay buried inside Ryder forever and forget the horrors of the world waiting for them outside their door. No peace was to be found in sleep; his normally unruffled dreams were now nightmares on the edge of insanity, keeping him awake in the hours before sunrise. He'd sit by Gemma's bed, the tears he couldn't shed during the day sliding down his face in the dim moonlight.

And so he did what he'd done since they fell in love: he held on to Ryder and loved him with all his heart, knowing whatever happened they'd have each other to hold.

"God." He couldn't catch his breath to gasp out more than a single word, and he meant it not only reverently for their incredible lovemaking, but also offered up as a plea.

"Jase?" Ryder's lips moved against his cheek.

"Yeah?"

"I'm sorry if I was too hard on you. No matter what decision I make, I'm always thinking about us and our marriage. You have to believe that."

The last thing Jason wanted to think or talk about while he lay in bed with Ryder was Ryder's mother. So to keep the peace, he kissed Ryder's cheek, his voice light.

"I know. I'm fine. Whatever we have to do for Gem."

He pulled out, and they went to the bathroom to shower and clean up. They'd just finished getting dressed when from the hallway they heard Ryder's cell phone ringing. As now was common, they froze for a moment, and Jason wondered if he'd ever hear a phone ring and not fear the worst. Ryder took off, scrambling for his phone.

Jason stood rooted in place, his heart banging, until he heard Ryder speak.

"Hi, Dad."

With those two words, his world settled back into focus, and Jason took a breath. He gave Ryder's shoulder a squeeze as he passed by him in the hallway on his way to the kitchen to see what he could scrounge up to eat. They'd been on such a crazy-ass schedule neither of them had found time to go grocery shopping, so the last thing he expected was to find the refrigerator stocked with fresh milk, juice, plastic containers of food, and a host of side dishes from mashed potatoes to vegetables and bagged salads. Recognizing his mother's precise handwriting, Jason teared up, knowing how many hours she'd spent at the hospital yet still found the time to come home to cook and get this to them.

His stomach rumbled, and he pulled out a container of roasted chicken cut up into pieces as well as two ears of corn and a bag of salad. Frankly, he was thrilled to eat something besides pizza and take-out Chinese. It wasn't until he saw Ryder pulling on his jacket that he stopped what he was doing and joined him in the hallway.

"Where are you going?"

Ryder slipped his cell phone, keys, and wallet in his pocket. "I'm meeting Landon and my father. We're going to my mother's apartment to talk to her."

What the hell? "Wait, you're going with them? I thought—"

"I gotta go, babe. They sent a car for me, and it's outside. I'll call you later."

And with a swift kiss he was gone, the door closing with a bang on its hinges. Unable to process what had happened, Jason walked back into the kitchen, his hunger gone, replaced by a sense of angry impotence. Before he could stop himself he picked up a glass and threw it against the wall. Chest heaving in frustration, he watched it smash to pieces, finding little satisfaction in his burst of childish anger.

Chapter Seven

THIRTY MINUTES OF fidgeting later, Ryder exited the black car onto Park Avenue. He stepped through the front doors of the luxury pre-war building he once lived in, and he wondered if the doormen he knew as a child still worked there.

"Ry."

Landon beckoned from underneath the green canopy.

"Hey." He managed a weak smile even as his stomach twisted into knots. "Thanks for being here." They hugged, and it still surprised Ryder that his little brother now matched him in height. "Is Dad here yet?"

"He's inside."

Ryder peered over Landon's shoulder and spied his father standing at the concierge desk, talking on the house phone. Knowing his mother was on the other end of that conversation sent a spurt of nerves through him.

"Uh," he said, his mouth suddenly too dry to speak. "I, uh—"

"Come on, Ry. It'll be all right. We're here with

you. She can't hurt you."

Overwhelmed with love for his brother, Ryder recognized his foolishness. He was a man, and she was his mother. Five years ago she'd hurt him more than he ever thought possible by wishing he wasn't her son. He no longer cared if she wanted him in her life. The only thing that mattered was Gemma and getting her the help she needed.

"You're right. This is about Gemma, not me. Not Jason."

"He's okay now with you being here without him, right?" Landon held the door open, and he passed by him and entered the once familiar lobby of his childhood home.

"Yeah, he's fine with it. No problems." Recalling their lovemaking before he left, Ryder's blood warmed. He couldn't have gotten any luckier than to have a man like Jason.

Watching them walk inside, his father spoke forcefully into the phone, then handed it to the young man in uniform behind the marble-topped desk.

"Good to see you outside of the hospital."

They hugged, Ryder once again thankful that at least he had some of his family to lean on. While he loved Jason's parents, it meant the world to him to have his father and brother by his side, giving their support and love as well. Family should care about each other.

"It's good to finally be out of there. I feel horrible even thinking that, seeing how Gemma is stuck there."

His father glanced at his watch. "As far as I know, she and Denise are watching their second or third mermaid movie. Denise said she'll stay there until Gemma falls asleep, and then I'll go pick her up."

"Thanks, Dad." The words came out choked, his throat too tight from holding back all the emotion swelling inside him. Love, fear, pain. It all mixed up into a deadly cocktail, and from his trembling, Ryder sensed he might be a breath away from losing his shit.

"No need to thank me. It's what family does. I may have been a lousy father to both of you, but I intend to make it up to my grandchildren." His father squeezed his shoulder. "Are you ready?"

"Does she know I'm here?"

His father nodded, and they began walking to the elevators, past the staggering crystal chandelier in the center of the room, past the collection of elegant, dainty furniture grouped in front of the fireplace with the oil painting of an idyllic East River scene. Nothing had changed in this rarified air since he'd last been here, yet everything was completely different. He'd found himself, found love, and become a father. Ryder wasn't the same man who faced down his mother in Jason's trailer—it all seemed like a lifetime ago.

"Yes." His father pressed the button to ring for the elevator. "She demanded to know why, but I merely said she'd have to wait for you to tell her." The door opened, revealing the elevator operator who'd been there since he was a child.

"Hello, Grady. How are you?" He shook the elderly man's hand.

"Well, I'll be damned. Good to see you, Ryder." His dark eyes twinkled. "Going up to see the dragon-lady?" His gaze flickered to Ryder's father. "I'm sorry, sir. I didn't mean to be disrespectful."

A smile curved his father's lips. "Don't worry about it. I'm not."

Ryder met Grady's eyes and gave him a reassuring grin. "It's nothing we haven't always thought. And I like that name."

THEY ALL LAUGHED, and like that, his nervousness evaporated. As horrible as everything was in his life now, he had his husband and his father and brother. He'd do what he had to do and never need to see his mother again.

"Yeah. We have some things to discuss."

"Well," said Grady, and he stopped the elevator on the twenty-second floor. "I know you lawyer types are persuasive. Don't leave until you get what you came for." He pulled the iron security gate to the side and the elevator door slid open. "I'll see you later, then."

"Thanks. See you later."

Feeling more like he walked toward an execution or to give an argument before a judge, Ryder followed in his father and brother's wake, their footsteps muffled by the plush carpeted floor. His father rang the illuminated bell, and Ryder could hear soft chimes playing inside the apartment. Despite his earlier confidence, he trembled. As if sensing his unease, Landon bumped his shoulder.

"Together, bro."

Ryder gave him a shaky smile.

The door opened, and for the first time in what seemed like forever, Ryder stood in the same space as his mother.

"I don't know what is of such life-or-death importance you needed to intrude upon my evening."

"You'll find out soon enough, Astrid." Without a care, his father swept past her and headed inside.

"Hello, Mother." Landon didn't leave his side.

They locked eyes, and with no satisfaction Ryder noted her drawn appearance. Always thin and impeccably dressed, she now looked more fragile, almost breakable. Every bone in her face stuck out in a sharp angle, and dark shadows lay like bruises beneath her eyes.

"Ryder." She stepped aside. "Come in, you and Landon, please."

He didn't expect a welcoming smile, but still Ryder counted her invitation to be a good sign. They all walked farther into the spacious apartment and took seats in the living room. He sat between his father and brother on the delicate antique sofa, while she chose a more formal chair, facing them. Once again Ryder was struck by her fragility, the bones in her legs sticking out in stark relief against her skin. He wondered if she was well. He wondered why he cared.

"I don't understand what you're all doing here. Ryder and I said everything we needed to the last time we were together."

The coldness hadn't changed, nor had the pinched lines of anger around her mouth softened.

"Things change."

She fixed him with a familiar flinty gaze. "Nothing's changed as far as I'm concerned."

"That's fine for you. Then you can sit there and listen to me and not talk." With his daughter's life on the line, Ryder wasn't about to take bullshit from anyone, least of all his own mother.

"Though you choose to ignore it, I am married to a wonderful man and we have a daughter. A beautiful little girl named Gemma."

"You named your daughter after my mother?"

"We named her after my grandmother. Gemma is a joy, and Jason and I love her with all our hearts. But she's sick now, and we need your help."

Something flickered for a moment in her eyes, and if Ryder believed she had a heart or a soul, he'd say it was pain and shock. Surely he must be mistaken.

"How can I help your child? She isn't even related to me."

"Once again you're letting your ugly prejudice and ignorance show. She *is* related to you, to us." He motioned to his father and Landon. "She's my biological child; we had her DNA tested. But why should that matter anyway? She's a helpless, defenseless child who's never done anything to you except be born and only knows the goodness in people. And right now I'm doing what I never thought I'd have to do."

He walked over to her chair and squatted down beside her. "I'm begging you, Mother, please. If you ever loved me or any of us, put aside your feelings about my sexuality and think about this little girl lying alone in a hospital bed tonight. Right now." He pulled out a picture of Gemma dressed up in her princess outfit last Halloween and thrust it into her hands. "This is your granddaughter, Mother. She's going to die if you don't help me. Help me save my daughter's life. I need you—she needs you."

He held his breath and waited, watching her at first look everywhere but the picture of Gemma, then finally glance down. Her eyes widened, then filled with tears.

"She's very pretty."

"She's beautiful," said his father from the sofa. "Smart and sweet-natured. Jason and Ryder are doing a wonderful job raising her."

With a shaking finger, his mother touched the picture, tracing Gemma's face. "She looks like you and Landon did when you were babies." Then, as if catching herself, she handed the picture back to him, a sorrowful expression in her eyes. "I'm sorry she's ill, but I don't see how I can help. I'm sure you have the best doctors, so—"

"She needs a bone-marrow transplant. She has a rare kind of anemia, and the only way to save her is with a transplant. We've all been tested already, and none of us are a match, not even me." He inhaled, then let out his breath, forcing himself to remain calm. "I need you to get tested. You're our last hope."

Her pale eyes widened in shock. "Tested? If you're not a match and you're her biological father, surely I'm not going to be a better match."

Disbelieving, he stared at her. "Are you turning me down?" He held up the picture. "You're willing to let my little girl die for your stupid, ugly prejudice?"

"Astrid. Surely you aren't saying no. Not even you could be that cruel." His father jumped up from his seat and stalked over to them. Ryder remained hunkered down on his heels, uncertain he had the ability to stand without falling over.

"For God's sake, Mom. She's an innocent child." Landon rose from his seat. "Are you a monster? How can you refuse?"

Placing her hands over her ears, she crouched within herself. "Stop attacking me."

"Then do the right thing and help my daughter."

Once again they locked gazes, and Ryder's heart lurched in his chest. For a moment he thought he caught a glimpse of the mother he had once loved before everything turned ugly.

"Yes, all right, I-I'll do it. Contrary to what you and your brother think, I'm not a monster or a terrible person. I have feelings. I'm sorry your daughter is ill, Ryder. I would never wish an innocent child harm."

He stood and gazed down on her sitting in her

chair. "Only your innocent son, whose only crime is in loving a man and not a woman, though, right?" Before she could answer, Ryder held up his hand. "I'm sorry. I swore to myself I wasn't going to say anything. This night wasn't meant to be about me and you and past hurts. It's about Gemma. I have the doctor's number here for you to call." He handed his mother Dr. Fleischer's card. "You can call her first thing in the morning to set up an appointment. It doesn't take long; it's only a swab."

It all happened so fast Ryder never even had time to remove his jacket. There was nothing left for him to say, and he wanted to go home, hold Jason and tell him everything.

"Thank you, Mother. I appreciate you putting aside our differences for Gemma."

His mother gave him a brief nod and sat staring off into space, twirling the card between her fingers. When they walked outside and he closed the door behind him, Ryder began to tremble.

"Wait. I can't..." Overwhelmed, he began to weep. The tears slid down his face, and he sank down, his shaking legs unable to support him. "Oh my God. She said yes. I can't believe it." He buried his face in his hands.

In an instant Landon was by his side. "It's going to be fine. I have a good feeling about it. You'll see. Gem will come out of this well and healthy."

Nodding in the comfort of his brother's embrace,

Ryder felt drained and curiously alone. As much as he loved his brother and father and needed them with him here tonight for their unquestioning support, it wasn't right.

He wanted Jason.

"I'm sorry. I didn't mean to get all emotional." He wiped his wet eyes with the sleeve of his jacket. "It's like everything came to a head and crashed down on me."

"It's understandable. Seeing her again was bad enough; having to plead for her help couldn't have been easy."

He stood, and his father hugged him. "I'm proud of you. You handled it perfectly."

"I just want to go home. I need to be with Jason."

All the way down in the elevator and even in the car ride home, Ryder replayed the events of the evening over and over in his head. How old his mother looked now, frail and defeated. Little remained of the ice-queen personality he'd last seen in Jason's trailer all those years ago. Ryder wondered if she regretted the choices she made that brought her to this point: alone, bitter, with no family or loved ones to share her life. And though he knew Jason would think him crazy, he couldn't help feel sorry for her sitting in that big apartment with nothing but ghosts whispering to her from the past.

The car pulled up in front of his house, and he barely let it come to a full stop before he unlocked the door and jumped out. From the large bay window, he could see the glow of the kitchen light in the back of the house, and his excitement grew. He couldn't wait to tell Jason everything.

"Babe," he called out. "I'm home."

When he received no answer, he went searching for Jason, only to find him asleep, slumped over the kitchen table, his cheek resting on his folded arms. Poor guy. He never had a moment's rest; between worrying about the business and Gemma's illness, Jason needed to relax. And Ryder knew exactly how to take care of his husband.

"Jase, wake up. I'm home." He slid his arms around him and kissed the back of his neck, anticipating a hot shower and whatever else came along with it.

"Did she say yes?" Without returning the kiss, Jason disengaged himself and stood, rubbing his eyes and blinking.

"Yes. She did. She's going to call tomorrow. I can't believe—"

"Good." Jason cut him off. "I'm going to bed." He turned his back and walked out of the kitchen and up the stairs.

Still in his jacket, Ryder followed him down the hall to their bedroom. "Don't you want to hear how it went?"

In the middle of pulling his T-shirt off, Jason didn't speak until he stood bare-chested. "Not really. I'm only interested that she's helping Gemma. Other than that, nothing she has to say is important to me unless she accepts me and our marriage." He slipped off his jeans, climbed into bed, and clicked off the lamp on his side of the bed, leaving Ryder in darkness.

"What the hell is going on?"

"You want to know what's going on?" Jason sat up and clicked on the light. "You keep saying what you're doing is for us, to help Gemma. But I'm a part of 'us,' and the three of us are a family. You running off to talk to her without including me in any decision-making makes it seem like I'm an afterthought."

"An afterthought?" Stunned, Ryder sat on the bed. "Everything I do I stop to think about how it will impact us as a family. I didn't want there to be more conflict. I swear that's all." The bed sagged beneath his weight as he inched closer to Jason, who remained stiff and unyielding. "Why can't you see that?"

A small sigh escaped Jason. "I dunno. Everything's changed so quickly. I don't feel like we're on the same page anymore."

Ryder could have said they hadn't been on the same page even before Gemma got sick; Jason's crazy work schedule had them living almost two separate lives. But he held back, not wanting to stoke the flames of an argument he had the chance to end. At least the dark anger had faded from Jason's face, and Ryder slid closer to hold him tight.

"It'll all be okay." Ryder pulled Jason close, the feel and scent of his skin as familiar as his own. They loved each other, and everything would work out. It had to.

Chapter Eight

"YOU'RE BEING A dick." Liam unwrapped his sandwich and bit into it, chewing noisily. "And I mean that in the nicest way possible."

Having little to no appetite, he'd still accepted Liam's invitation to lunch in the hospital cafeteria to escape Ryder's attempts to corner him and talk. The previous night was the first time he'd gone to bed angry with Ryder since their marriage, and feeling miserable and cowardly, Jason woke extra early and snuck out of the house to come to the hospital. Thank God Emily and Connor had the dogs for now, although he missed them and planned to go there tonight for a long walk and some quality snuggle time.

Pushing his tray out of the way, he muttered, "Screw you. I am not." But even that sounded halfhearted. He knew how childishly he was behaving, but he couldn't help feeling incredibly hurt over last night's events. "Why can't you see how I feel? Ryder made such a big deal of needing to talk to his mother by himself. He even called me a distraction. And then to find out he went with his father and brother made me feel even worse."

"Why?" Liam set his sandwich down, his brow furrowed. "I'm not surprised."

Damn. Didn't anyone see his side of things?

"I'm his husband, and I wanted to be there for him. He should've wanted me for support."

"But your wanting it doesn't make it right." Liam opened his sandwich and frowned. "I told them no tomato. Look," said Liam, tossing the half-eaten sandwich aside. "I said you're being a dick because you're stuck on it being about you. There's alotta history with that family that I bet even you don't know about. Ryder's lived with a ton of bullshit and hurt. Who better to understand it than his father and brother? Plus you would be a distraction to that bitch. She hates you. Why dredge those feelings up? Ryder did what he had to do."

"Everything you said makes sense. And I know it. But he never once said he'd be going with Alexander and Landon. When he told me he needed to do it by himself, to me that meant alone, with no one else. Then to find he planned all along to go with them shocked me, and I guess I overreacted."

"You guess?" Liam quirked a brow and leaned back in his chair, folding his arms. Over the years, he and Liam had grown closer than ever, their families taking weekend trips to the beach or mountains. When they all came together for holidays, Jason wondered how he would have managed without his parents and brothers and sisters, and it hit him that by shutting Ryder out, he acted no better than Ryder's mother.

"I've been a dick."

"Lightbulb moment, huh?" Liam smirked and picked up his sandwich again. "You can thank me later."

"Shit. I gotta go." He stood and without saying good-bye, ran out of the cafeteria. He needed to find Ryder and apologize for—as Liam had put it so succinctly—being a dick. Waiting impatiently by the elevator, he looked at this phone, not paying attention when the doors opened. He walked inside and ran right into someone.

"Excuse me, I'm sorry. I…"

The words dried in his throat. Standing before him was Ryder's mother.

"Mrs. Daniels." He stepped aside to let her out. "I'm sorry, I hope I didn't hurt you. I wasn't paying attention."

In her designer suit and perfectly styled hair, at first glance Astrid Daniels looked the same as she did five years earlier when she stood in his trailer, lashing out at him. Staring at her more intently though, Jason could see the web of fine lines scoring her pale skin and the dark shadows under her eyes. Little remained of the inimitable woman who'd confronted him.

"I'm quite all right. If you'll excuse me, I have an appointment." She walked away, her posture stiff and straight.

"Thank you, Mrs. Daniels," he called after her. "Ryder and I appreciate what you're doing."

Her steps faltered, and she stopped and looked back over her shoulder.

"Contrary to what you think about me, I'm neither a monster nor an evil person. My personal feelings about you have no bearing on the life of an innocent child."

"I'm glad to hear that. And still, I have to say thank you. You're our last hope now for a family match, and I wanted to let you know I appreciate you doing this."

Tilting her head in acknowledgment, she gave him a slightly thawed-out smile. "I don't want to be late." And with that she hurried down the corridor, her heels tapping on the linoleum floor.

She turned the corner and disappeared from sight. Her footsteps faded into the distance and Jason stood, staring after her. He sighed and shook his head. "I don't understand people."

"Me either."

Jason spun around to face an unsmiling Ryder, who leaned against the wall, his face slack with fatigue.

"Oh, hi."

"Is that all you have to say?" Ryder advanced several steps but stopped short of coming close enough to touch. "Oh, hi? You snuck out before I woke up, and you've been avoiding me all day."

His face flamed with heat, but Ryder had him pegged perfectly and wouldn't give him any leeway.

"Yeah, what do you think, I don't know you and

how you react in certain situations? When you don't want to talk about something you run away."

"I—I've been a shit."

Ryder said nothing, and Jason propped himself against the wall. "I feel so lost. You tell me how much you need to do it on your own, and then I find out that you went with Alexander and Landon. I'm not upset. At least not anymore."

"What happened to change your mind?"

His lip twitched, holding back a smile. "I had a talk with Liam, and he told me I was being a dick."

"I guess once again I owe Liam a thank-you."

The years fell away, and for a moment Jason remembered how scared and alone he'd been at the beginning of his relationship with Ryder. Questioning his bisexuality, wondering if he was really in love with a man, he ran away and hid from everyone until Liam came to find him and turned him upside down with the truth. He loved Ryder and nothing and nobody could ever change that. He'd thought he'd moved past the point of needing his older brother to spell things out for him, but in a way it made Jason happy to know how much Liam cared.

"It isn't like that. I know I'm being stupid, but I can't help it. Before I met you, I was standing still in life, but once I had you, I could move ahead. I needed you to get me from point A to point B. Now here I am, back again, stuck spinning my wheels in the mud, unable to move. Scared to death this time. But I never stopped needing you. I never will."

"Nothing's changed, Jase. We're still the same people we were before this horrible disease of Gemma's knocked us on our asses. I'll never stop needing you either." Ryder closed in on him, the heat rolling off his body to envelop Jason in its warmth. "We can't let this tear us apart."

"Never," said Jason, sliding his arms around Ryder's waist. "I won't let it."

They stood for a moment, foreheads pressed together, drawing strength from each other as they had throughout the years. Recognizing how foolish he'd been, Jason vowed not to let petty insecurities rule his head and instead listen to his heart, which had yet to steer him wrong from the first time he met Ryder.

"I'm sorry."

"Okay. And I promise to talk to you more about everything that happens."

Conscious that they were in a public place, Jason held off on pinning Ryder up against the wall and kissing him senseless and instead ran his fingers down Ryder's jaw. "Hey. I love you, you know."

"I know." The glow that had been missing in Ryder's eyes returned. "Love you too."

Then Jason remembered something he hadn't told Ryder. "Your mom's here. I ran into her." He laughed. "Close your mouth."

As if in a daze, Ryder complied, but that did nothing to erase the shock from his face. "You saw her? She spoke to you?" He looked at his watch. "It's not April Fools' is it?"

"You're a regular comedian. No, it isn't, and I have to say, I know it had to bother her, but she did speak to me."

"Was she at least cordial? Damn her. Even if she is helping Gem, I won't let her treat you like a piece of shit."

The elevator doors opened, and a noisy group spilled out. Jason grabbed Ryder's hand, pulled him inside once it cleared out, and punched the button. The doors slid closed, and they were alone.

"It was fine. I had to thank her. Because even though she refuses to acknowledge me, she may be the one to save our daughter's life, and I will be the bigger person and show her I'm good enough for you."

A frown tugged Ryder's lips downward. "Don't say that. It's ridiculous for you to even let that thought cross your mind. She's the one with the problem, remember. Not you, or me." He raked his hand through his hair. "I've never understood it, but I've given up trying."

"She told me that she's not a monster or an evil person." Recalling Ryder's pain at being cut off from his family and the elaborate lies his mother told to keep him away from his father and brother, Jason had good cause to dispute that. Now that he'd experienced fatherhood and the absolute selfless devotion that went into parenting, any mother who denied her child was a monster in his eyes. He'd rather die than cause Gemma any pain.

"I'm shocked she spoke to you."

The elevator bounced to a stop on Gemma's floor, and they exited the cab. Jason took Ryder's hand and gave it a squeeze.

"I may have forced her hand, but who cares? As long as she helps our daughter, I don't care what she says. She can call me a rainbow fucking unicorn for all that her opinion means to me."

Ryder stopped short, causing Jason to run right into him.

"Don't say that."

"But it's true. She has no ability to hurt me because I don't care about her. It's your opinion that matters to me, not hers. Once she's done with the test, I don't expect her to be a presence in our lives."

Seeing the flash of darkness in Ryder's eyes, Jason slipped his arm around Ryder's waist to hold him closer. "I'm sorry, babe. I wish it weren't so for your sake, 'cause it kills me seeing you twisted in knots about it for so many years. I know how you've tortured yourself and it upsets me."

"All I wanted was for her to care about me."

Jason rubbed Ryder's back to soothe him. "Maybe this will change things, and that taking the test means she's opened the door for you."

Without speaking, they began walking again down the long hospital corridor. Though Gemma's diagnosis happened only a little over a week ago, to Jason, these walls and more inexplicably the sounds and smells of the hospital had become frighteningly familiar. An involuntary shudder rippled through him. He'd always hated hospitals. Before they entered Gemma's room they stopped to gaze at the scene in front of them.

Jason's entire family surrounded Gemma. Mark and Liam, along with Landon, sat in chairs next to her bed, entertaining her with her stuffed dogs, while his sister and his mother read her stories and painted her nails. Alexander sat with his father, discussing something in the newspaper. And somewhere in the bowels of this hospital, Ryder's mother waited to get tested, the fate of his daughter's life and everyone's happiness resting with her.

They remained in the doorway and spoke in hushed tones. "I don't think I have to deal with it. She made it pretty clear last night that she had no desire to get to know Gemma or you. The only reason she's doing this is probably to settle her own conscience. I mean, who could say no to helping a defenseless child?"

"Like she said to me, she's no monster."

Gemma spied them from her bed. "Daddy Ry, Daddy Jay, look at my nails. They're all sparkly."

She wiggled her fingers in the air, and Jason's heart squeezed painfully tight. How could Astrid Daniels not want to be a part of this child's life? What drove her to such disapproval and disgust that she was willing to give up her entire family to be alone? He had zero patience and time to figure that woman out—not when his child needed him.

"Hey, baby doll. You look gorgeous." He dropped Ryder's hand and swept to her side, giving her kisses all over her face and causing her to dissolve into delighted giggles. "Maybe Nana should do mine too."

Gemma squealed. "Oh yes, you and Daddy Ry. Please?"

"Of course." Ryder stood on the other side of her bed and met his eyes over Gemma's head. "Let's do our nails like Gem's, and we won't take it off until she comes home."

"I'll do mine too," said Jessie. "And I'll tell Nic up at school to paint hers as well."

"Yay." Gemma bounced in her bed. "We'll all match. You too, Nana."

"Of course." His mother shook up the bottle and started painting his nails with the tiny brush.

"Jase, what's going on? Getting a manicure?" Liam set the fuzzy stuffed animal on the foot of Gemma's bed. "You gonna do your toes too?"

"It's for Gemma. We're going to keep the polish on our nails until she comes home. Like a show of support."

Liam's gaze flickered over to Gemma, who gave him an excited grin. "Isn't it pretty?" She showed him her hands, and Liam gave her a strangely poignant smile.

"It sure is, sweetheart." He circled the foot of the bed to stand next to Jason, who'd taken a seat next to his mother. "Hey, Ma. Do mine next." He flexed his hand, showing off his work-roughened fingers.

Whoa, what? "Dude, you don't have to do that. You're on-site. It's okay. We know you love her."

A smile curved Liam's lips. "Don't tell me what the f—" At his mother's kick to his shins Liam caught himself in mid-curse. "Uh, sorry, Ma. Don't tell me what I shouldn't do. It's for my niece and goddaughter. I'll do anything to make her happy. Even wear nail polish."

Christ, he was going to break down and start crying in front of everyone. "Thanks."

Liam ruffled his hair, like he used to do when Jason was a child. "Anything for you guys."

"Well, don't leave us out, right guys?" Mark held out his hand. "I want to wear it too."

"I'm game," said Landon, joining them. "Anything for Gem."

His manicure finished, Jason watched as his mother applied a thin coat to Ryder's nails and then Liam's. Landon and Mark stood waiting their turn, and Jason left the bedside and joined his father and Alexander on the opposite side of the room.

"What was going on there? Looked like a party." Alexander folded up his newspaper. "I have to go soon and get ready for a pre-trial conference."

"We're all getting our nails painted in solidarity for Gemma, and we won't take off the polish until she comes home." He held out his hands and spread his fingers wide. "It's not so bad, see?"

For a moment Alexander stared at his hands, and Jason wondered if he'd gone too far. Having a gay son-in-law was one thing, but Jason suspected his staid, conservative father-in-law might not like his son and son-in-law wearing rainbow, sparkly nail polish.

"Gemma couldn't have asked for better parents than you and Ryder."

Overcome, Jason had to swallow past the lump in his throat. "Th-thanks. That means a lot to both of us."

"It's the truth. I wish I could've been there for my children like you both are with Gemma. But I've been trying with her. I hope Ryder can see that."

"We both do. She loves you and Denise."

Once again, Alexander's gaze flitted to his hands, and a brief smile ghosted across his lips. "I always said I'd do anything for her." He stood, and Jason watched as he approached the crowd at Gemma's bedside and held out his hands.

"I'd like to get my nails done too, Helen."

Stunned, Jason caught Ryder's equally shocked expression. A delighted smile burst across his face. Maybe Ryder still hadn't been certain of his father's acceptance, but seeing him get his nails painted while he casually chatted with Gemma should finally put all those bad memories to rest for good.

"I hope your mother's got enough polish for me," said his father. "I'm not gonna be the only one left out."

If only everything was as simple as wearing sparkly nail polish.

Chapter Nine

"STILL NO WORD yet, no." Ryder paced up and down the hall, the dogs underfoot. It had been four days of torture waiting for his mother's test results. After spending the morning and afternoon with Gemma they left the hospital a bit early—Jason's parents had ordered them to go home for a while—and took the dogs from Emily and Connor. To say Pearl and Trouper had been happy to see him and Jason was an understatement—they hadn't left their sides for a moment, and it was comical to wake up and find two eighty-pound dogs in their bed, crowding up next to them.

"I know. I'll make sure you know as soon as we do. Okay, bye." He hung up with his father and tossed the phone on the chair. "Come here, you two." He sank down to his knees, and the dogs swarmed him, licking his face and whining with repressed glee. Their tails whipped back and forth. "Let's go to the back and play ball." They'd arranged that Jason would leave early to meet his parents at the hospital, while he'd bring the dogs to Connor and Emily's house, then go to Gemma.

They jumped up and down around him, barking as if they understood, which Ryder firmly believed they did. He grabbed their toys and some treats and headed outside through the back door. From the front of the house, one would never expect it to have such a nice-sized backyard, especially in the city, but two years ago their neighbor sold them his much smaller house, and they knocked it down to give them the extra room they wanted for the dogs and a play space for Gemma and any other children they might want to have. After the construction and reconfiguration, the fenced-in lot was a good eighty-by-a-hundred square feet and made for some excellent games of fetch.

One sweaty hour later, they tumbled back inside, the dogs immediately going for the bowls of fresh water Ryder poured out for them before taking a bottle from the refrigerator for himself. He left them slurping and headed into the shower. Feeling renewed and invigorated, he checked his cell phone, alarmed to see he had three missed calls from Dr. Fleischer in the short time he was in the shower and getting dressed.

He pressed the button to redial and got her secretary.

"Dr. Fleischer's office."

"Hi, Naomi, this is Ryder Daniels returning her call."

"Oh, Ryder, yes, hold on. I know she was trying to reach you."

Before he could ask anything further, she put him

on hold. Was something wrong with Gemma? Was she worse? Ryder chewed his lip, angry at himself and guilty they'd left her to check on the dogs and catch up on some work.

"Ryder?" Roberta, as she told them to call her, clicked on. "Are you there?"

"Yes, Roberta. What is it, is ev—"

"She's a match, Ryder. Your mother is a match for Gemma for the bone-marrow transplant."

Pinpoints of light circled his eyes, and he found it hard to catch his breath. With a thump he sat on the floor. The dogs ran into his bedroom, probably thinking this was a game, and settled down around him. As usual, Pearl nudged her way into his lap, giving him comfort and security.

"Are you sure? This isn't a mistake, right?" The phone beeped with call waiting and Ryder saw it was Jason.

"No. Not at all. She's a match. When I called and couldn't get you, I contacted Jason. My ears are still recovering from his reaction."

Surreal would be the best term to describe his state of being at the moment. How ironic. Of everyone in their families tested, the one person who disapproved of Gemma even being born was the one they now had to ask for help, to give her a second chance at life.

"I-I almost don't know what to say."

"I understand." The sympathy in Roberta's voice was apparent even over the phone. "Do you want me to call her, or do you want to tell her?"

"I think it's best coming from you." Ryder laid his cheek against Pearl's head. "I'm not sure if she'd believe me, and this way it's more official."

"I'm happy to do it." She hesitated. "You know, Ryder, sometimes these types of things bring families together."

Not this time. "Thanks, Roberta. I appreciate it. What happens now? When do we do the transplant?"

"We have to do a medical screening on your mother and make sure she's healthy to donate immediately. And, we're going to have to ask her if she wants to. Her taking the test is only the start. She has to agree to be Gemma's donor and then go through the procedure of bone-marrow withdrawal."

A terrible thought entered his mind as he stroked Pearl's silky ears. "What if she changes her mind and decides not to go through with it?" As unbearably cruel as it might be, Ryder couldn't anticipate his mother's behavior.

"Let's not think the worst. I'm going to call her right now, and I'm sure you want to tell everyone else."

"You're right. Thanks so much. This might be one of the best days of my life."

Hopefully his mother would agree and not turn it into the worst.

He hit Speed Dial, and Jason picked up.

"Ry!"

"I was on the phone with Roberta. I can't believe it."

"I can't stop laughing and crying at the same time."

Tears rushed to his eyes. "I know. I thought I was going to faint, but now I can't stop smiling. I'm on my way to the hospital right now. Meet you there?"

"Yeah. We were in Gem's room having breakfast, and my mom screamed so loud the security guard rushed in. Hold on a sec."

Ryder couldn't help but laugh. The cloudy mist around everything faded, bringing the world back into sparkling clarity. The sound of muffled voices reached him through the phone, but Ryder couldn't make out the words.

Laughing, Jason came back on the phone. "We're getting some coffee now. They said they have to do a few more tests on Gem. Mom says she loves you and to give you a kiss from her." In a whisper meant only for his ears, Jason continued. "I think I can arrange that. And I have some personal kisses to give to you as well to make up for lost time."

"We both do," said Ryder. "I've missed you, missed us."

"Me too," answered Jason. "So damn much. See you soon, babe. I love you."

Immediately upon hanging up, Ryder called his father's office and got his secretary.

"Ryder, your father's in a meeting."

"Tell him I'm on the phone with news. He'll want to take the call."

"Is it about Gemma?" Her voice rose with excitement.

"I can't say yet."

"Oh. Of course. I'll get him right away."

In a moment, his father came on the phone. "Ryder? What is it? Janet said you had news."

"She's a match. Mom's a match. I just got the call from the doctor."

"Thank God." Knowing his father was at the office, it shocked Ryder to hear him crying openly into the phone.

"It's going to be okay, Dad."

"I'm sorry; it's overwhelming after all these days of hoping, disappointments, and waiting."

"I almost passed out when she told me. I'm going to drop the dogs off with Connor and Emily, then head over to the hospital."

"Definitely. And Ryder?"

"Yeah?"

"I love you."

From absolute misery comes ultimate joy. "I love you too."

He disconnected the call and put down the phone. "Come here, you two." He held out his arms to his dogs, and Trouper and Pearl crowded into his lap. Ryder hugged them tight. Everything would be okay.

"DO YOU THINK she's going to do it, Ry?" Emily poured him a cup of coffee and set a plate of bagels on the table in front of him, along with a platter of lox, cream cheese, tomatoes, and onions. "Have something to eat before you run off. You look like you've lost weight."

Connor reached for a bagel, and Emily swatted at his hand. "You don't have that problem, buddy-boy. This is for Ryder."

"Hey, I work hard." Connor winked, and Emily rolled her eyes but handed him the plate. "Take half. You don't need more."

With a smug smile, Connor took half of a bagel, slathered on the cream cheese, and plopped a hunk of lox on it. "I didn't hear any complaints last night. Besides, more of me to love." He took a huge bite, chewing noisily.

"Insufferable." But she smiled as she said it.

For all that his world had turned upside down with Gemma's illness, it was nice to see that some things never changed. No matter what, these were his people.

"And to answer your question. She'd better. I'm not going to walk away from her like I did when she rejected me. I'll fucking tie her down and take the bone marrow myself if she forces me to."

Emily regarded him with sympathy creasing her face. "I can't imagine she'd say no. What would be the point of testing in the first place?"

He gulped down his coffee and wrapped a bagel in a napkin to eat in the car. "Who knows what's in her head? I've given up trying to figure her out. But I swear she'd better not mess with Jason or me, else Connor may have to come bail us both out of jail." He gave her a kiss and waved to Connor, who gave him the thumbs-up. The dogs, perhaps sensing this had become a familiar routine for them, waited patiently by his side. He felt so bad neglecting them, but there was little he could do right now, and once again he didn't know what he'd do without his friends.

"I'm sorry, you two. Jason and I promise to make it up to you when this is all over. Be good."

He hugged them close, accepting their sloppy kisses, then, after wiping his face with a paper towel Emily handed him, headed out the door to the car waiting at the curb. Typically, he preferred the train, but with Gemma so sick, Ryder had no patience to wait on overcrowded platforms and accepted his father's offer of a car. Any means necessary to get him to Gemma as quickly as possible.

The ride into the city flew by swiftly, but Ryder still had time to take care of some pressing problems he'd been neglecting at the office. Once Gemma received the transplant and it hopefully worked, things could get back to normal for them. Ryder had to believe it would be so. Any other outcome would be too terrible to imagine. He jotted some notes on his tablet to reference later in the day when he checked in with the office.

The now-familiar hospital building loomed in front of him, and he shoved his tablet into his messenger bag.

"Thanks, Ricky."

"Take care, Ryder. Give your daughter a hug from

me. Tell her I have a spot saved in the front seat right next to me when she's ready."

"Will do." He slammed the door shut and took the steps two at a time. He couldn't wait to see Gemma and Jason so they could finally discuss the next steps in her treatment. The guards, all familiar faces by now, greeted him warmly with wide smiles.

"Great morning, huh, Ryder?"

"Good news travels fast, I see," he said, giving their raised hands high-fives. "I'll see you guys later."

Feeling more lighthearted than he had in weeks, Ryder walked inside the hospital which now didn't seem as forbidding and ominous as it once did. Funny how in one moment your life can change from good to bad, then flip back again. Even the elevator ride took no time at all, and Ryder hurried down the corridor to Gemma's room.

"Hey, baby girl. How—"

A sight he never thought would come to pass greeted him. There sat his mother, dressed in her designer suit, perched on the edge of a chair, not too close but close enough to the side of the hospital bed. While Gemma's face radiated all smiles, Ryder knew his mother and sensed her discomfort.

"Daddy Ry, look."

Giving her smooth cheek a kiss, Ryder hugged her tight. "I see. How are you?"

Like a puppy, she squirmed and wriggled in his arms. "You're squishing me."

He loosened his grip but didn't release his hold on her, keeping her tucked into his chest, feeling as though he had to protect her from his mother.

"Aren't you going to say hi? That's your mommy, right?"

Mommy. If ever a woman didn't fit that term of endearment, it was his mother. "Well," he said, using the time to gather his thoughts. "Right now I'm saying hi to you." When he could no longer put it off, he let Gemma go and sat down on the side of her bed. "Hello, Mother."

"Ryder." In a surprising show of nerves, his mother's thin fingers twisted the leather straps of a handbag that probably cost almost as much as Gemma's preschool tuition. "I had a call from Dr. Fleischer's office."

"I'm aware."

"Daddy, Grandma said she's going to help make me better so I can go home."

His heart pounded. A child shouldn't have to hear discussions about saving their life. It wasn't right, but then so much of what happened in life wasn't fair or right. "You're going to do it?" Ryder needed that validation from her, that she'd agreed to help him.

"Yes. I signed the forms this morning and have a physical scheduled in an hour, where they'll do extensive blood work." Her hands stilled. "I couldn't get her face out of my mind after you showed me her picture."

Giving Gemma one last kiss, he stood from his perch on her bed. "I'll be right back, honey. I need to talk to Grandma." God that sounded odd, calling his mother Grandma.

The nurse walked in, creating the perfect diversion for him. "We can step outside while the nurse takes care of Gemma." He watched his mother gather her purse and led the way out of the room, around the corner to an alcove where they could talk with some degree of privacy.

"I appreciate what you're doing to help Gemma." An ironic twist, to have to thank his mother for anything. But he couldn't risk her wrath. Not when Gemma's life depended on her.

"I never thought I'd have children, never mind a grandchild." The icy veneer around her melted a bit. "She's so innocent and shouldn't have to suffer for the mistakes of adults."

"Her being my daughter is not a mistake. My loving Jason and our marriage isn't one either."

At the mention of Jason, her lips tightened. "It can't be easy for you two raising a child."

At that, Ryder quirked a brow. "Your concern is overwhelming, Mother. Are you offering to babysit?"

"There's no need to taunt me. I am helping you."

He bit his tongue, holding back everything he wanted to say, every name he longed to call her but couldn't. He needed her, and that was the hardest pill to swallow.

"Yes, you are, and I thank you."

She tilted her head in acknowledgment. "You're welcome."

The nurse peeked around the corner. "Ryder? You can go back inside now. We're all finished, and she's asking for you."

"Thanks, Evelyn." In Ryder's mind, there was little left to say to his mother. "I have to get back to her."

"I'll be leaving, then."

"Oh, Mrs. Daniels, Gemma asked if you could say good-bye to her also."

Her pencil-thin brows shot up in surprise, and to Ryder's disbelief, she smiled. Her first real smile, Ryder suspected, in a long time. "Yes. Of course I will."

Following his mother down the corridor, Ryder worried what he'd tell Jason when he saw him. Rightfully so, Jason would be pissed at Ryder's mother for using Gemma's illness as a mechanism to see her without approving of their relationship, marriage, or even Gemma's birth. At the sight of Jason and his parents in Gemma's room, Ryder held his breath, hoping his mother wouldn't behave like the reactionary she was and make snide or derogatory comments, but he needn't have worried. True to her nature, his mother never spoke to those she deemed not worthy, and Jason's parents, down-to-earth and understanding of their son's sexuality and marriage, certainly didn't measure up to her standards. She ignored everyone; in her mind no one else mattered save for herself and Gemma.

To her credit, and because she was a classy woman, Helen stood and greeted her anyway.

"Hello, Mrs. Daniels. I'm Helen Mallory, Jason's

mother, and this is my husband, Anthony."

Tony, more of a grudge holder against anyone he perceived slighted a member of his family, didn't join his wife in standing but merely tilted his head.

Would she even answer? Manners dictated she at least respond, but Ryder didn't know his mother anymore, if he ever did. And even after all this time, it saddened him to think it took a sick child for her to speak to him. Was it some internal flaw that made him still long to understand her and wish she could accept him?

"Good morning," his mother said in response, her chilly tone as off-putting as any words might have been. She turned her back and stood by Gemma's bed, looking down at her with a curious yet almost frightened expression. "You wanted to say good-bye to me?"

Ryder stole a quick glance at Helen, who pursed her lips as if she wanted to say more but sat down. Tony whispered in her ear, but she shook her head. Ryder walked over to his in-laws and gave them each a welcoming hug.

"Daddy Jay always says it's not nice to leave without saying good-bye." Round blue eyes studied his mother's face. "Thank you for helping me not be sick anymore."

Damn. He and Jason thought they'd done such a good job of shielding Gemma from the worst of it, but she knew. How could she not, with all the tests and needles she's endured? Pain stabbed through him, and he had to turn away, even as Jason's arms came around to hold him up. Like always, Jason was there when he needed him the most.

"Hey, you. I'm here, and it's gonna be fine. She's going to beat this. Gem's a tough cookie, like her daddy."

Giving him a somewhat watery smile, Ryder leaned into him, and that electric current, always alive between the two of them, warmed his soul. With Jason by his side, they could beat the world. "The last thing I expected was to find my mother sitting next to Gem's bed. I wanted to throw her out, but we need her. I'm sorry," he whispered.

Noticing her pointedly ignoring him and Jason, he watched as she gave Gemma a hesitant kiss on the forehead, and with her back soldier-straight, walk out of the room without saying good-bye to him or anyone else.

What happened to a person to make them so cold and unforgiving? Children weren't born with a capacity to hate. And though Ryder didn't remember all that much about his grandmother, he recalled her easy smile to everyone and kindness to the birds they fed at her summer home in Connecticut, making him all the more curious to understand his mother's resistance to him and his child.

Jason hugged him closer. "Don't worry about it. You have nothing to feel sorry for. She's the one missing out on a wonderful grandchild like Gem." His lips curved in a wicked grin. "Not to mention a stellar son-in-law like myself."

God, he loved Jason. No one else had the ability to make him smile and forget his problems more than this man. His heart lighter than only a moment before, Ryder allowed himself a brief laugh before sobering. "She said she never thought she'd have children or grandchildren. What do you make of that?"

"Who knows. Your mother is someone I never had any desire to figure out. She hates me without even knowing me. That's kind of hard to take, like a punch in the gut."

"I know, and I'm sorry. It's not my fault, yet I feel like I'm constantly making excuses for her. But you know what's really important?" He faced Jason. "I love you. And that's never going to change."

"Right back at you, babe." Jason kissed him.

"Daddy Jay, Daddy Ry. I want a kiss too," called Gemma from across the room. She sat in bed and held her arms out wide. "Please?"

Who could blame his mother for wanting to see Gemma? She was adorable.

They joined Gemma, each snuggling up to a side.

"It's a peanut butter and Gemma sandwich," said Jason, laughing his head off.

"Oh, brother." Ryder leaned over to whisper in Gemma's ear. "Your Daddy is such a dork."

Chapter Ten

JASON HURRIED DOWN the steps, having gotten the text that his car was outside. For the past week, he and Ryder had barely left the hospital. Gemma had undergone chemo and radiation to clean her marrow in preparation for the transplant. Once Ryder's mother had proved to be a match for the bone-marrow transplant, she'd undergone a battery of exams. She'd passed them all, yet Jason still didn't believe she meant to go through with the procedure, until Ryder informed him that the actual harvesting of the bone marrow was in the morning. To his absolute shock, Ryder insisted on being there for the procedure. His excuse was that he wanted to make sure it went off without any problems, but Jason knew better. His softhearted and softheaded husband continued to hold out hope for a relationship with a woman who had yet to show any remorse for her past behavior toward them both.

Despite the good news of the match and that Gemma had a chance for a real recovery, when they came home from the hospital he and Jason got into a terrible fight about his mother.

"I'm not saying she'll change overnight. I'm looking to see if there is any way to start anew. Your own brother hated me initially, remember?" Ryder poked his finger at Jason's chest.

Astonished, Jason stood there, his anger building. "Are you fucking kidding me? You have the nerve to put my brother and your mother in the same sentence and compare them?"

"Why not?" Ryder folded his arms and glared, sparks shooting from his eyes. "He called me almost every disgusting name in the book. And it took John, a stranger, to make him see what an asshole he'd been. Why can't you accept that my mother could have the same change of heart?"

Biting his tongue, Jason really wanted to say, *Because she's a cold, heartless bitch who never cared about you or anyone*. Luckily he controlled himself because he loved Ryder and knew how much those words would hurt him. Instead he took Ryder around and held him close, hating how stiff and unyielding Ryder felt in his arms.

"I'm not saying she can't. I'm saying that it's been over five years of silence, and it took a desperately sick child to force her back into our lives."

"You think I'm being foolish, I know. I'm not an idiot. I know most likely it won't change a thing. But maybe seeing Gemma will soften her a bit. If anyone could, a child can. Sometimes a crisis is necessary to make people see what's really important. Like when

John used his own brother's death to force Liam to face his bad behavior."

Arguing with a lawyer never worked, in his opinion. Ryder possessed a mind that recalled the tiniest details, and Jason had little desire to end up in a war of words with him. None of it helped them or Gemma.

"Let's not compare wrongs. We're lucky Liam realized how mistaken he was and things are good between us all, right? You've never said you still hold it against him, Ry."

"I don't, really."

But Ryder's hesitation indicated he held something back, and Jason stayed silent, waiting for Ryder to finish.

"It hurt, though, and yeah, we're good now. I love Liam and don't doubt he loves and supports us. But that doesn't mean I've forgotten. And I'm not saying you should forget my mother's horrible treatment of you and us. But she's all alone, Jase, and the procedure's under general anesthesia. Someone should be with her, and Landon is in the middle of midterms. I'm already going to be there in the hospital for Gem, so..." He buried his face in Jason's neck. "I know you think I'm an asshole, but—"

"It's okay. You're my asshole, and one of the reasons I love you is your kind and generous heart."

Ryder shook with laughter. "I should say thanks, but I think I'll hold off." He stepped back and met Jason's eyes. "If you really don't want me to be there, I won't."

But Jason knew Ryder didn't mean it and only said it to avoid confrontation. He couldn't put that kind of pressure on Ryder. "It'll be okay."

And today it was.

Ryder had left early to go to the hospital, promising to meet Jason when the harvesting was done. Never a fan of hospitals himself, Jason tapped his feet nervously as the elevator creaked its way up to Gemma's new room in the pediatric cancer ward. The first person he saw when he stepped out of the elevator was Liam.

"Jase. I just got here. I went to her old room, but they said they moved Gemma up here. What's going on? Where's Ryder?"

Shoulder to shoulder they walked down the hospital corridor to Gemma's room. "Because she had to have chemo and radiation, they moved her to the cancer ward. And Ryder's in the surgical waiting area while they do the harvesting for the bone marrow on his mother."

"What's he doing there?" Liam stopped short. "Wait. He's gonna be there with *her*?"

He understood Liam's astonishment; he'd had the same attitude, but Ryder was his husband and had his loyalty. Jason wasn't about to let anyone, not even his own brother, give Ryder any grief.

"We discussed it. Ryder has his reasons, and I support him."

"You've gotta be kidding me." Liam stepped in front of him, his eyes bugged out with astonishment. "Why the hell would he be there with her instead of with his daughter where he belongs?"

It took every ounce of Jason's strength not to punch his brother through the wall. "Let me say this slowly and carefully so you'll understand and I never have to repeat it. Don't you ever, EVER question Ryder's love or dedication to Gemma or to me. We don't need your approval, and I don't have to explain to you why we do what we do. Got it?"

When Liam opened his mouth, Jason shook his head. "I'm telling you, think before you speak. 'Cause if you're going to argue with me, get the fuck out of my face."

Liam stared at him for a moment, then nodded. "I'm sorry. I didn't mean that the way it sounded. I know how much Ryder loves Gemma. It bugs the shit outta me that he wastes his time on his bitch of a mother. Ma told me how she ignored her and Dad that day she showed up at the hospital. It burns my gut."

They'd continued walking, and Jason empathized with his brother. He too wanted Ryder to forget about Astrid Daniels but knew Ryder's innate goodness wouldn't allow it. Jason knew Ryder secretly wished for that happy ending with his mother that unfortunately would never come to pass.

"Let him do what he has to, and don't pass judgment. None of us know what we'd do if we were in the same situation. All I can do is be there to support him."

"You're right." Liam sighed. "I can't imagine all the

shit Ryder's been through. And now this. I'm sorry, Jase. I didn't mean to put even more of a burden on you."

"It's okay. I know it's coming from a good place."

Things had changed drastically between yesterday and today. The special isolation room they'd moved her to had large red warning signs stating No Visitors Allowed plastered on the doors and walls, and through the window Jason could see the heavily gowned and masked nurses tending to Gemma.

His once laughing, bright-eyed girl lay quiet and pale in her bed, and Jason turned away, his insides heaving. "Oh God. I'm gonna be sick." Liam grabbed him and hugged him hard.

"Steady, Jase. You're doing this to save her life."

Knowing it was one thing. Seeing firsthand what the chemicals did to her made him want to vomit. More than ever he wanted Ryder and wished he was there with him.

He nodded into his brother's chest, grateful to have him there but still scared to death. All these weeks now seemed like a dream, being here with Gem, keeping her laughing and unafraid. Even when they gave her the chemo treatment, she'd been so brave and barely cried. The reality now hit him hard, knocking the breath from his body. Watching them check the catheter line that would feed her the life-saving stem cells, seeing them adjust her IV drip, it painted a picture of the gruesome reality his child now lived. Her absolute courage astounded him.

"I told Mom and Dad not to come today and used the excuse of asking them to take the dogs from Emily and Connor. I can't have them see her like this; it would kill them."

"Man, what are you gonna do about the dogs?"

"They're going to stay with Mom and Dad for now. Because of her suppressed immune system after the transplant, Gem can't have them in the house; everyone who visits her for the time being will have to wear a mask and gloves. As a matter of fact, that reminds me: we have to get a service in to sanitize our house before she comes home." He pulled out his phone and made a note.

"How long before she can come home?" Liam leaned against the wall while watching through the window. "You must be ready."

"Yeah." Jason walked over to the row of hard plastic chairs and slumped into one, stretching his legs in front of him. "I want to grab her and carry her home right now, but the doctors all tell us at least another month. They have to give her these anti-rejection drugs and make sure the transplant takes and that she's progressing."

Liam slanted him a look, and Jason read his unanswered questions: *What if all this doesn't work? What then?* Jason refused to acknowledge that possibility. He thought back to the summer that now seemed like years ago. How carefree they'd been, laughing and playing as if they hadn't a worry in the world. How foolish they'd been to think ugliness could never come and touch them, when all along it had waited in the wings, mocking them.

"Mr. Mallory?" A nurse stood before him. "Would you like to come in and say hi?"

Careful not to knock her over, Jason jumped out of his chair. "Of course, yes. Please. I definitely do." He knew he babbled, but the nerves had taken control. Somewhere in this hospital, Ryder's mother held the key not only to Gemma's life but his and Ryder's. The control freak he was, Jason hated not being able to do anything but sit and wait for test results and outcomes and for other people to take care of his child.

"First put this gown on, please; then cover your head." She handed him the garments.

Cocooning himself in the gown, relief poured through Jason as Ryder's familiar figure turned the corner from down the far corridor. The burden that only moments ago seemed too much to bear lightened at the sight of his husband. No one set his world to rights like Ryder.

"Hey, you." Ryder, breathing heavily, bent over to kiss his cheek. "What's going on?" He walked over to the window and after staring inside for a moment, turned back with a frightened face. "What's wrong? She looks awful."

"It's the chemo and radiation. No matter that it's going to help her, it's poison." Jason held the mask in his shaking hand. He wanted to punch the wall. "Is the other part done?"

"Yeah. Thank you." Ryder accepted a gown for himself from the nurse and slipped it on as they spoke. "She's in recovery and will have to stay overnight. So that's over with. I stayed long enough to make sure she came out of the anesthesia and to speak to the doctor. The harvesting was successful."

Jason noticed Liam stayed back, on the other side of the waiting area, giving them personal space. "Liam's here, but he's not allowed inside. Only immediate family."

Ryder slipped his mask on, fixing the loops behind his ears, then waved over at Liam, who gave him a halfhearted smile and a wave. "Yeah, of course. I told my dad and Denise not to even come today."

Jason slipped his own mask on and after being led to a sink where they scrubbed down with antibacterial soap, they put on their gloves and entered the room. Asleep now, Gemma lay still and peaceful, her face smooth and unlined.

Jason felt Ryder's hand creep into his and gave it a squeeze. "It's going to be okay." He had to believe that, otherwise he wouldn't be able to get up in the morning. "There's so much love here for her it can't possibly not work out."

"Emily said she bought a special candle and some crystals and was channeling all this healing light to Gemma. I used to laugh at her, but no more."

"Nope. We'll take whatever we can get."

ONE WEEK POST-TRANSPLANT and the doctors were cautiously optimistic about Gemma's progress. The transplant hadn't shown signs of rejection, and she could sit up for longer periods of time without feeling sick. Both he and Ryder had been staying at the hospital round-the-clock, with only brief forays back home to shower and change, and if he looked anything like Ryder, they needed to slow down or they'd be admitted to the hospital themselves. Neither had eaten a decent meal since her diagnosis, and there were times when he relieved Ryder at the hospital or vice versa so that they merely passed each other early in the morning or late at night, with barely a kiss or a tired greeting between them.

The strain now showed on them both, and Jason awakened, surprised to find Ryder lying next to him. He struggled to remember the last time they woke up together. "Hey, you." He nudged Ryder's bare shoulder. "Are you up?"

"Yeah." Ryder rolled over on his back to stare up at the ceiling. "I'm so wiped. Maybe I'm coming down with something. My head is pounding."

"Hmm," Jason said, touching his head. "You're not warm. But you can't go see Gem if you feel like this. Stay in bed, drink hot tea, and get some chicken soup."

"Yes, dear," Ryder said with a tired smile. "You

sound like your mother."

"Oh, babe," said Jason, crawling on top of him. "My mother has no place in our bedroom." He kissed Ryder's neck, and hearing his sigh of pleasure, pressed his lips against the rapidly beating pulse. The two of them had rarely gone two days without making love since they'd married, and Jason missed the simple closeness of cuddling in bed. Nowadays, it seemed they were never on the same wavelength or even in the same zip code.

"That feels so good," Ryder murmured. "Helps my head stop aching."

"I ache for you. All over." Jason straddled him. "I've missed you so damn much."

He brushed his lips over Ryder's. *Too fucking long.* Spending time with Ryder now, to find their way back to each other, didn't take time away from Gemma. They needed this. His parents planned to stop by the hospital to see Gemma, even if they couldn't go into her room.

"I've missed you too and our nights together." Ryder wrapped his arms around Jason and held him closer, and Jason smiled against his cheek. "I love you."

Jason skimmed the pads of his fingers over Ryder's face. "You are so important to me. Everything I am, everything I've ever wanted, I've accomplished because I have you by my side. Don't ever slip away from me." He slid down, smoothing his hands over Ryder's skin, and pulled off the comforter.

"I couldn't. Losing you would be like losing myself."

At the sight of Ryder lying naked beneath him, the aforementioned ache blossomed into a blaze of hunger. He swirled his tongue around Ryder's pointed nipples, then sucked them. Excitement, lust, and need throbbed in thick, heavy beats through his blood, and Jason quivered, on the edge of breaking apart. He trailed wet kisses down Ryder's chest and abdomen, his lips coming to rest on the glistening tip of Ryder's cock.

Ryder sighed his pleasure. "God, babe."

Without answering, Jason licked around the wide head, then slid his tongue down the thick shaft to bury his face in the golden, springy hair of Ryder's groin. Ryder moaned and spread his legs.

"Come on."

Sitting up on his knees, Jason gazed down at Ryder lying flushed and spread-eagled on the bed. Nearly dizzy from desire, he scrambled to the night table for the lube. Quickly slicking his erection, Jason picked up one of Ryder's legs, folding it to his chest, and stared at Ryder's pink hole.

"Fuck, I love watching myself slide into you." He slapped his dick against Ryder's ass, and Ryder groaned louder than before.

"Do it already," said Ryder through gritted teeth.

Holding his breath, Jason pushed inside, snapping his hips to slide deep, knowing Ryder wanted what he did—completeness, to be whole. And now, with their family bruised but not broken, they could reconnect the circle and be intact once again. Making love, joining their bodies, gave them both that feeling of infinity. A love unbroken.

"God, Ry." The air shimmered around him, the mad rush of sensation gathering beneath his skin, drawing his body tight, then exploding, sending him shattering to pieces. Everything was the same, yet different; Ryder's body opened beneath him, accepting and welcoming, then held him in a fiercely clinging, heated clasp.

He buried his face in Ryder's neck, and once again Ryder drew him close, fingers digging into the meat of his shoulders as if he couldn't pull him near enough. Ryder shuddered, and Jason sensed the wetness of his husband's climax between their sweat-slicked bodies.

"I love you." Ryder surprised him by nipping at his neck, marking Jason's skin with his tongue and lips. "My headache is almost gone. You're a wizard."

Jason laughed and pulled out of Ryder. "Let's take a shower. I think you should rest a bit; you still look a little pale. I'll go to the hospital now and see Gem." He rolled out of bed, and Ryder joined him. Arm in arm, they walked to the bathroom, where Jason washed himself first, then took care of Ryder and once he dried him off, tucked Ryder back into bed.

"Don't get out of bed. Try and get some sleep, and I'll be back soon."

"I like it when you get all bossy," said Ryder with a smile that turned into a huge yawn.

"Sleep." Jason turned out the light and hurried down the stairs, anxious now to get to the hospital. Without the dogs and Gemma playing and making a racket, the house seemed too big for the two of them, and Jason hated it.

An hour later, with more of a spring in his step than he'd had in weeks, Jason strode down the hospital corridor to Gemma's room. He turned the corner and stopped short. There, at the window, looking into Gemma's room, stood Ryder's mother.

They'd not heard a word from her since the transplant, and Jason had hoped she'd stay out of their lives. Seeing her here now, Jason steeled himself for an unpleasant discussion.

"Mrs. Daniels."

Years ago, slightly intimidated by her wealth and arrogance, Jason might have held his tongue. No longer.

"What are you doing here?"

"I should think that would be obvious. I'm seeing my grandchild."

Furious that this woman thought she could step into their lives without any need to apologize for her behavior to him and the isolation and—as Jason saw it—abuse of her son, Jason planted his feet, folded his arms, and glared at her.

"You don't have that right. Not without our permission."

And to his surprise, she laughed. "Who are you to tell me no? Ryder is her father, not you."

He would not lose it here in the hospital. Swallowing his anger and hurt, Jason spoke through gritted teeth. "Not that I need to explain anything to you, but I adopted Gemma. Ryder and I both are her parents in every way."

Nonplussed, her gaze returned to Gemma. "I didn't know that was allowed. It could never have happened when I was younger. We had to follow what society expected of us. It wasn't right."

"We're human beings like everyone else. We have the right to love who we want, get married, and have families. People have no right to tell us it's wrong."

"It was a different time back then, and expectations were different. Now, perhaps you're right." Her fingertips touched the window. "She's a lovely child."

"We love her very much. She's our whole world." This surreal conversation contained undertones of something more. Some bigger picture Jason hadn't yet grasped and didn't have time for. Gemma, not Ryder's mother, was his main concern, and it was time for him to cut this short. The time had come for Astrid Daniels to hear the truth.

"While we appreciate what you did for Gemma, that doesn't negate how you've treated Ryder all his life. I don't care whether you like me or not, even though for all our sakes it would be nice to get along. But Ryder cares. For some reason he holds out hope that you'll accept him, even though I know you won't."

"It's not that simple."

Astonished, Jason couldn't help his bitterness. "Of course it is. He's your child. You're supposed to love him and accept his life and his family. Because like it or not, Gemma and I are his family. And until you admit that to yourself and make peace, you can't see her. As one of her fathers, I do have that right, and I'm executing it."

Without waiting for a reaction or response, Jason donned a robe, mask, and gloves and entered Gemma's room, keeping his back turned to the window. He smiled down at Gemma, who for the first time since the treatment had a bit of color in her cheeks.

"How do you feel, baby?"

"Okay, I guess."

Soon they'd bring her home, and he swore never to take anything in his life for granted. Life was too precious a gift. Too bad Ryder's mother didn't understand that. He snuck a look over his shoulder and wasn't surprised to see her gone. Obviously she would rather hold on to her bitterness and hate. He had his family to hold on to, and he planned to never let them go.

Chapter Eleven

"I STILL CAN'T believe she's finally home." Ryder stood with Jason in the doorway to Gemma's room, staring at her sweet, sleeping face. "Even though it's been over a week, I sometimes wake up and peek in her room, thinking I must've dreamed it. There were times I thought we'd never see it happen, you know? This past month of waiting to see if the marrow was going to be rejected was the scariest month of my life."

"Yeah," said Jason quietly, leaning up against the door, his gaze fixed on Gemma as well. "Mine too. She's still a little weak, but I see the difference, don't you?"

"I do. And I'm not saying that to grasp at straws. There's a spark in her eyes I haven't seen since even before her diagnosis. Maybe that's a good sign." Keeping as silent as possible, he tiptoed over to the side of her bed to turn off the little dog-shaped lamp on her nightstand. He returned to Jason and closed the door three-quarters of the way as they left the room. "Being home and in her own bed can only help her. Let's let her sleep."

Keeping as silent as possible, they went downstairs to the kitchen, where Jason took two beers from the refrigerator, popped the tops, and handed him one.

"I feel like we haven't had a chance to take a deep breath in so long and really talk."

"Thanks. You're right. Now that Gem's settled back at home we can start getting our life back in order, I hope. Even with the doctor appointments, she'll be here with us." The one thing he missed most was quiet time with Jason, where, after they'd put Gemma to bed, the two of them would stretch out together on the sofa and talk about their respective days. "Want to go hang out in the living room, put on a movie and make out?"

An uneasy feeling settled in the pit of Ryder's stomach when Jason failed to even crack a smile. "What's wrong, babe?"

"I have to tell you something, and I hope you don't get mad at me."

Ryder set the bottle down on the table without taking a sip. "Why don't I like the sound of that? What is it? You crashed your truck?" But his joke fell flat when Jason didn't laugh along with him. "You're scaring me, Jase. What's wrong?"

"Um right after Gemma had her transplant, I went to the hospital and you stayed home; you weren't feeling well, remember?"

This sounded random, but Jason looked too serious for his liking. "Yeah. Kind of. I mean, it was over a month ago, but I remember you went. So what?" There it went again, the guilty expression on his face coupled with those dark-blue eyes that looked anywhere and everywhere but at him. "What is it?"

"I, uh, ran into your mother. She stopped by to see Gemma."

If Jason had said he'd run into the President, Ryder couldn't have been more shocked. "My *mother*? Are you sure? No, that was dumb, of course you are. You spoke to her?"

"Yeah. I told her that while we could never thank her enough for saving Gemma's life, she first had to accept us as a married couple. Only then would we discuss her seeing Gemma."

Thoughts flew round and round Ryder's head, making him dizzy with a combination of wonder, fear, and sadness. What did it say about her as a person that it took a gravely ill child to get his mother to acknowledge his existence and act like a decent human being?

"Why didn't you tell me before now?"

Fidgeting, he waited for Jason to finish taking a drink. "Gemma getting better was my main focus and with everything else going on, I honestly forgot. I'm sorry, Ry. My mother called me earlier to check on how Gem was feeling, and suddenly it popped into my head and I knew I had to tell you right away."

"Did she seem receptive?"

Jason shrugged and made circles on the placemat with the bottom of his beer bottle. "Who could tell? She made these cryptic remarks like it was easier now than it was back then, and expectations were different." His brows pinched together in thought. "We never really talked about allowing her into Gemma's life. I never thought she'd want it. When she appeared, my automatic response was to say no."

"We need to talk about it now, then."

Wide-eyed, Jason stared at him like he had two heads. "You're not considering it, are you?"

Oddly enough, he was; Jason's tone only made him more defensive.

"Why not? If she's willing to change."

"I don't think she will. Look," said Jason, gesturing with the beer bottle. "Since I saw her at the hospital until now she hasn't called you or made any attempt to find out how Gemma is, right? That says it all to me."

"Jason," Ryder said, trying to keep his tone reasonable. Hard to do when the subject was his mother. In all their years together, it remained the one sore spot in their relationship. "Why would she? You told her to stay away."

"So now it's my fault?" The hurt and defensiveness in Jason's voice rang out, echoing in the quiet kitchen.

"Shh. Keep it down; you'll wake Gemma. You're overreacting like you always do every time my mother comes up." He braced his elbows on the table. "I never said it was your fault. But I'm going to have to talk to her. To see if she's willing to change, you know?"

"You're kidding, right? I mean, we don't need her approval for our marriage, our life, right?"

Of course, Jason already knew the answer. "No, but—"

"And now Gem's been home a week and it's been over a month since you saw her at the hospital and still nothing from her. So that's it. She hasn't changed, and she thought she could bully her way to get what she wants."

As usual Jason thought he knew what was best, especially when it came to his mother. Ryder refused to fight with Jason about this. Nothing would ever change Jason's mind. But no matter what Jason believed he knew, this was a decision Ryder needed to make on his own. And what did his mother mean when she said it wasn't as easy back then? What did she know about being gay?

All his life, from when he was a child, Ryder knew he was attracted to boys; he also knew he had to hide it from his school friends, who thought being gay meant he wanted to have sex with any man he saw. His first sexual encounter in the locker room was both glorious and terrifying; the first touch to his body left him breathless and aching, dizzy with a hunger he'd only imagined. Until the boy warned him that if Ryder told anyone what happened or looked at him in the hallways, he'd deny it and have his football team friends beat the crap out of him.

So Ryder kept silent, finding sex but always wishing for love.

He came out to his family because he couldn't live

inside himself any longer. He needed people to turn to; people he could count on. He always expected it to be his family. But at ten years younger than him, Landon was too little at that point to understand fully, and his father, forever tired and busy with the firm, merely looked confused and said nothing, spending even longer hours at work. It was left up to his mother, a person who should always love you and be there for you, to reassure him that everything would be fine and no matter what, he would be loved. Instead, she railed against him and refused to accept it—first by throwing every available girl in his path, and when that didn't work, cutting him off from his family entirely.

That time spent virtually alone, with only Connor and Emily and stolen time with Landon, changed him, making him afraid of abandonment and loss. And even knowing how much Jason loved him, Ryder often gave in rather than standing up and fighting for something he wanted, simply because he valued peace and calm. Maybe deep in his heart, he feared Jason would walk away and disappear.

"I, I don't want to talk about it now," Ryder said weakly, pushing away from the table. Yeah, he was acting the coward, but the last thing he wanted was a fight with Jason. Because if they kept talking, that's what would happen. To Ryder, discovering his mother had actually visited Gemma on her own, plus her odd remarks to Jason, could only mean she might be willing to bend her harsh stance and come to some agreement.

Which meant he needed to see his mother and find out what—if any—role she thought to play in his daughter's life, and set the ground rules if she chose to be involved.

"Babe, believe me, the last thing I want to do is talk about your mother. She hasn't given any indication she's willing to accept you as gay or me as your husband, so there's nothing to say." Finishing off his beer, Jason stood and grabbed him around the waist as he passed by. "Now how about that make-out session you mentioned earlier?"

Giving Jason a halfhearted smile, Ryder allowed Jason to lead him to the sofa where they spent the next hour kissing and driving each other wild with pleasure, yet for the first time, Ryder didn't drift off to a sated, peaceful sleep. Even after he and Jason went upstairs to bed, rest eluded him, and Ryder spent half the night staring at the wall. Finally, as the clock hit four a.m., Ryder fell asleep, but not before he'd made the decision to go see his mother.

WITH A GUILTY pang, he left Jason at home. Helen would be coming by to "see her baby," and Ryder had no doubt Gemma would be well taken care of. They'd held off on visitors to let Gemma get used to being at home and gather more strength. Erica had gotten another job but still vowed to come back once Gemma was recovered and able to attend school again.

Helen came prepared with videos of Pearl and

Trouper since the doctors said it would be another month before Gemma could be reintroduced to the dogs. To both his and Jason's amusement, Tony walked in behind her, carrying what looked to be half of a toy store.

Jason had no clue he planned to see his mother, but Ryder had grown tired of his "I'm right and you're wrong" attitude. Dammit, if he wanted to confront his mother, he had every right to do so.

"Gotta go, babe; I'll be home this afternoon." He gave Jason a hasty kiss good-bye, his hand on the front doorknob, not wanting to be stopped and questioned.

"Wait a sec. Ma," yelled Jason. "I told you not to buy her any more dolls. She has enough." Harried, he ran his hands through his hair. "She doesn't listen to me. It's like I'm talking to a wall."

"Have fun with that." Ryder laughed and escaped, leaving Jason to argue with his parents. He ran down the front steps, his heart banging against his chest, both from the thought of facing his mother and the secret he kept from Jason. Neither one made him feel very good about himself. He slid into the back seat of the waiting limo and reclined, closing his eyes as the car bumped along the streets.

The way he saw it, he came out a loser either way. Maybe he should have brought Jason with him to face his mother shoulder to shoulder to throw down the gauntlet: either accept their marriage or never see Gemma.

But he knew his mother. Where he was the type who hated conflict and confrontation and would rather give in than face discord, she drew strength, even thrived on arguments. All Ryder could see was her throwing out chilly insults, then sitting back, enjoying his struggle to control Jason's temper. He'd never get a chance to say his piece and find out why exactly she'd cut him out of her life so completely.

So instead he sat in the car, chewing his bottom lip, nerves blossoming, planning what to say to her, but in the end he gave up. He wanted to see how she acted toward him. They hadn't had a real conversation since that time in the hospital. After that he'd been caught up with Gemma's treatment, and everything else in his life had taken a back seat. By the time he thought to see his mother again, she'd retreated to the safety of her apartment.

The car turned up Park Avenue and stopped at a red light, several blocks away from her apartment building. This world of grand homes and luxury shops held no appeal to him—it never had—and living here seemed a lifetime ago. In truth it was a different life, one he had no desire to reclaim. His reality now centered on Sunday dinners, movie nights, and snuggling with Jason and Gemma on the sofa, creating memories, something he'd wished for as a child when he'd spent the majority of his time with nannies.

Family time didn't exist growing up here. When his mother did grace them with her presence at home, she very firmly placed herself behind an icy veneer he'd found impossible to penetrate. His father had worked late into the evening, and it wasn't unusual for Ryder to go weeks without catching a glimpse of him. It was the exception rather than the rule for him to be home for dinner.

The car pulled up in front of the gray stone façade of the apartment building, and immediately a doorman hurried over to open the car door.

"Good morning, sir."

He hadn't called ahead of time, knowing his mother would find a way to wiggle out of seeing him. A surprise attack would be best.

"Morning. Thank you."

The car drove off, and Ryder followed the doorman into the building, where he greeted the concierge with a friendly smile. If he stopped, the man would most likely call up and announce his presence, which Ryder didn't want, so he merely waved his greeting. Luckily the concierge was involved with a tenant complaining about construction noise, and because Ryder did at one time live there, the man didn't stop him. Ryder hurried down the marble hallway to the elevators, slipping into one seconds before the doors closed. He nodded to the unfamiliar elevator operator and took a deep breath in an attempt to regulate his pounding heart. Nerves skittered through him, and he adjusted his tie in the gilt-framed mirror. If he was to face his mother, he needed to be dressed in his armor. She'd not find fault with him for showing up lacking, in jeans and a sweatshirt.

He exited the elevator as the door to his mother's apartment closed behind a tall, patrician woman. Her graying hair, swept up on top of her head, revealed her elegant bone structure and a magnificent pair of pearl earrings. She looked to be about his mother's age, and Ryder knew he'd never seen her before.

She eyed him with interest, and he gave her a polite smile.

"Hello," he said and moved over so she could pass by in the somewhat narrow hallway.

Instead, to his shock, she placed a hand on his arm. "You're Ryder, Astrid's son. Am I correct?"

"Yes," he answered, wondering how she knew him. Most likely a crony from one of his mother's innumerable charities. "Have we met? I'm sorry. I don't think I've ever seen you before."

Her dark eyes stared at him with a mixture of tenderness and sorrow. "You look so much like her when Astrid and I were young; it's uncanny."

Ryder blinked in confusion. "You knew my mother growing up?" Aside from what his grandmother told him about their life in Connecticut, his mother never spoke of her childhood. His grandparents traveled the world, leaving his mother to be raised by governesses until she was old enough to send to boarding school. "Were you friends?" His mother had never mentioned being close with anyone, leading him to assume she'd always led a solitary life.

A smile flickered on her lips. “In a way. Our parents were very close, but I was taken out of boarding school and sent to Paris when I was almost seventeen and married there eventually. I’ve lived throughout Europe ever since. This is the first time I’ve been back in the States since my husband died last year.”

“I’m sorry.”

“I’m not.” Once again, the glimmer of a smile came and went. “He wasn’t the right person for me, but back then we did what we were told and married who your parents said was right for you. Not like today.”

Ryder blinked slowly, her words sinking in, sounding familiar to him. They echoed what his mother had told Jason when they’d spoken. “I’m sorry. I don’t even know your name.”

“Emmaline Heaton.”

“Nice to meet you, Emmaline.”

“The first thing I did once I got settled in at my hotel was look up your mother. It’s nice to have one friendly face.”

Ryder had a hard time imagining his mother as anyone’s friendly face, but he understood.

“Friends are important. So is family.”

“Yes,” she said, her eyes growing soft. “Astrid told me you’re married with a daughter. How is she doing?”

“She’s progressing, thank you. And yes, my husband’s name is Jason Mallory, and we’ve been married a little over five years.” He left out the fact that his mother refused to accept or even acknowledge his husband.

Her eyes glimmered. "I'm glad your daughter's doing well. And that you're happy."

They shared a smile, then she gave his arm another squeeze. "I have to run. It was wonderful meeting you. You should know, the two of you are more alike than you think."

Before he could react, she walked over to the elevator and pressed the button. The door opened, and he ran over to her. "Wait, what do you mean?"

She stepped inside the elevator cab and shook her head. "It's not my place. I'm glad I had the chance to meet you. Good-bye, Ryder."

The door closed in his face, and Ryder was left standing there with even more questions than before.

Chapter Twelve

WITH HIS HEART beating a painful tattoo, Ryder pressed the doorbell to his mother's apartment. He felt as though he'd been given a bag of riddles but no clue as to what questions to ask to solve them. At the sound of his mother's footsteps clicking on the wooden floors, he put the mystery woman from his mother's past out of his mind and waited.

"Did you forget something, Em—" Her voice died off. "Ryder. What are you doing here?"

The sight of her red-rimmed eyes shocked him, and he watched as she crumpled a tissue in her hand as if to hide it from him.

"May I come in?"

Her gaze darted over his shoulder.

"She's gone."

His mother remained cool, though he sensed a storm swirling under that rock-calm exterior. "What? Oh yes. She's an old acquaintance."

To his surprise, she opened the door, granting him entrance into the sprawling apartment. A housekeeper cleared the remains of what appeared to be two settings for tea in the formal living room. He waited until she left the room, then removed his coat and took a seat on the delicate wooden sofa. Thinking how Gemma loved to jump on their sofa at home, Ryder suppressed a smile. No jumping on the furniture in this apartment. An overwhelming desire seized him to go home and hug his husband and child.

His mother stood at the entrance to the room, immaculate as always, dressed in a gray suit with a crisp white blouse. Not a hair dared move out of place, but her skillfully applied makeup couldn't hide her turmoil. He couldn't explain it, but there was an emptiness about her he hadn't seen before. Like someone had blown out her fire and all that remained was the smoldering ash.

"Sit down. I came here to talk to you about something. But you don't have to lie to me." He crossed his ankle over his knee. "I know who she is."

His mother glanced at him sharply but didn't answer until she sat across from him in a spare, hardback chair, her spine stiff and straight.

"Who, Emmaline? We knew each other growing up. She's been living in Europe and thought to come say hello."

"Was she your best friend?"

"What brings you here?" She dodged his question, fear clouding her eyes. "It isn't Gemma, is it? Things are still going well with the transplant?"

Perhaps she did have a heart. "Gemma is fine; she

came home a week ago. I thought you might have kept in touch to make sure she was okay, but after a month passed I gave up hope." At his subtle dig, his mother's lips tightened, but he continued. "Obviously she tires easily, but we're keeping our fingers crossed the worst is over."

Looking down at the tissue she hadn't stopped shredding in her hands, his mother exhaled a ragged breath. "I'm glad." She met his steady gaze. "So what is it? I'm busy today and don't have time to sit about and talk."

"Don't you think it's time to put aside our differences for Gemma's sake?"

Her mouth thinned to an angry slash. "Nothing's changed." She rose to her feet. "Now if you'll excuse me…"

"Sit down." He surprised himself with the vehemence of his tone.

Her eyes widened, shock flaring in their pale-blue depths, yet she complied. "You have no right to speak to me that way."

"I have every right. I'm your son. And I know you have some heart because you went to see Gemma in the hospital."

Her brows drew up tight, like angry slashes on her pale skin. "He told you that?"

"*He* has a name," he said through gritted teeth. "Jason. His name is Jason Mallory, and he is my husband and Gemma's father. Gemma is *our* daughter."

"That child is pure Daniels. There is nothing of him in her, and she deserves to be brought up the right way."

Every time he thought he could have a normal conversation with her, she said things that made him lose his mind and want to choke some sense into her.

"He is her father as much as I am. Jason gives her all his goodness and kindness, his caring and compassion. She *is* being brought up the right way. In a house full of love and friendship, with laughter and kisses. Not the cold, unfeeling way we were brought up, by nannies and governesses, or shipped off to boarding school as soon as you could get rid of me. Why bother having children, goddamn it, if you didn't want us to begin with?"

Pale and shaking, she rose from her seat, hands clenched at her sides. "Because that's what we were supposed to do. I didn't want children; I never did. I never even wanted to be married." The ragged bits of tissue fell from her hand, fluttering to the floor. "Get out and leave me alone. You're able to live your life the way you want, the way I could never. Go live it and stop bothering me."

Sad and confused, Ryder watched his mother hurry out of the room, having come no closer to resolving the issue of her acceptance of his marriage and his life than before he arrived. He came to the conclusion that he'd been completely wrong to do this without Jason. The whole time here he hadn't felt right, and after the last time, when he went to his mother to ask for her help in donating bone marrow without telling Jason first, he'd promised Jason not to leave him out of any important conversations again. Now he'd have to go home to confess and hope Jason wouldn't blow up at him. Knowing how mulish and angry Jason became whenever the topic of his mother came up, Ryder sincerely doubted it but was ready to take full responsibility for his actions.

He rose to leave and spotting a pen lying on the rug, bent to pick it up. The elegant script read *St. Regis Hotel*, and he surmised his mother's earlier visitor, the mysterious Emmaline, had dropped it. Ryder slipped it into his pocket and gathered up his coat. With his hand on the doorknob, he looked back into the apartment he grew up in, knowing he'd most likely never return. Since before they were married, Jason had, in one way or another, told him his mother would never accept their marriage or change her feelings about his sexuality, and yet he'd clung to the childish hope that someday he'd be able to change her mind.

No longer. Ryder opened the door and walked out, closing it with a soft click behind him. Time to go home and be with the people who loved and cared for him. Some things weren't meant to be.

"JASE? I'M HOME." Almost an hour later, he walked through his front door. "Where are you?"

Helen came down the stairs. "Oh, good, you're back. Jason's been worried; he couldn't reach you." She removed her protective mask. "He ran out to the store to pick up a few things Gemma asked for."

Ryder kissed his mother-in-law's cheek. "Sorry. My phone died. I guess I forgot to charge it. How is she?"

A bright smile lit up Helen's face. "Oh, she's wonderful. Ate all her breakfast and sat up and played a while. She got a little tired, so I put her down for a nap right before you walked in. Dad will be back later on, and your father called. He said you can reach him at the office."

"Thanks." Ryder slung his coat over the banister, and he stood deep in thought. A frown tugged his lips downward.

"What's wrong? You look upset."

"I did something and I know Jason's going to be furious with me over it."

Helen beckoned to him. "Let's go into the kitchen."

He followed Helen and sat down at the round oak table. He recalled the day they brought baby Gemma home from the hospital, all swaddled in pink with only the tip of her nose showing through. They must've stayed up all night on either side of her crib, listening to her breathe, jumping at every move she made. In the corner, Gemma's high chair still lay folded up against the wall by the back door. Neither he nor Jason could bear to get rid of it or even move it to the garage, as it was their last holdover from her baby days. Her smiling face when she banged on the tray or dumped her food on the floor never failed to lift his heart.

"Coffee?" Helen raised the thermal carafe.

"Please." Elbows on the table, Ryder braced his chin in his hands and stared down at the table. "As long as I live I won't understand people who turn their backs on their family."

"Oh, honey, I know you hoped your mother would reconsider about everything." After she poured them two mugfuls, she sat down across from him. "I thought she would too, especially after she donated her bone marrow to Gemma. How could she not want to be a part of her own granddaughter's life?" She shook her head, then took a sip of her coffee.

The warmth of the coffee through the thick mug did little to dispel the coldness seeping through him since he left his mother's apartment. How many more times would he be forced to suffer through rejection before he understood that no matter what he did, or how much he pleaded, his mother had no desire to reconcile? Staring at Helen's warm and homey face, Ryder contemplated confessing about his meeting with his mother that morning. Maybe she'd be able to help him figure out where he went wrong.

"Can I talk to you about something?"

"Anything." She rose to come sit next to him and took his hand in hers, giving it a squeeze. "You're like my own child, Ryder. I couldn't love you any more than if I'd given birth to you."

"I went to see my mother this morning."

"Oh."

He could see the surprise and concern on her face.

"What's worse is that I didn't tell Jason, even though I promised I wouldn't keep things from him anymore. And he was right as usual. She's never going to change." The coffee forgotten, he pushed away from the table to pace the room. "Jason told me he found her outside Gemma's room after the transplant and she made some strange remarks. I wanted to make one last-ditch effort to see if I could appeal to her, for Gemma's sake."

"It didn't go as well as you hoped?" Compassion, not condemnation, resided in her eyes.

He shut his eyes for a moment, stemming the pain. "She never wanted children, she said. She never even wanted to be married. I don't understand anything about her, who she is and why she made the decision to live her life as she did."

"I'm sorry."

Helen rose from the table to give him a hug, and Ryder clung to her, unable to make sense of any of it.

"All along I thought the problem was me and my being gay, but it wasn't. It was her."

"That should give you some comfort at least. Nothing you could do would make her a different person." Helen led him back to the table, where they sat once again. "You're a wonderful man, Ryder. You're kind, you care about other people's feelings, and you love with all your heart. But sometimes you're too kind, and I see you giving in too easily to keep the peace."

He took a sip of the slightly cooled coffee and smiled over the rim. “I hate to fight. I’ve had enough of it to last me the rest of my life.”

“But you can’t let people walk all over you. I love my sons, but they like to get their own way.” Her lips curved in a wry smile. “It wouldn’t kill Jason to give in every once in a while.”

“He’s going to be furious when he finds out I went to see my mother and again I didn’t ask him to come.”

Her brow wrinkled. “May I ask why you didn’t, if you don’t mind answering?”

Ryder chose his words with care and deliberation, not wanting Helen to think he was bad-mouthing Jason, which he wasn’t.

“I always hoped somewhere in the future my mother would realize how wrong she was about me and my marriage and want to reconcile. Even when she didn’t show up at our wedding or for Gemma’s birth, I held out hope. I know Jason thought I was foolish, but something inside me couldn’t make that final cut between us.”

“She’s your mother. I understand that.”

Encouraged, Ryder continued, his voice rising in persuasion. “So when Jason told me she’d come to see Gemma, I thought, oh, here’s my chance, my in—if you want to call it that—to get to her and have that as my excuse. But he seemed so dismissive of her visit, and I didn’t want to have a fight about it…” He trailed off.

“So you went yourself rather than have a confrontation with him. Oh, Ryder, you should've talked to Jason about it first."

"Talked to me about what first?"

Jason breezed in, his arms filled with groceries.

Frozen with surprise, Ryder turned in mute appeal to Helen, who gave him a pointed look before walking over to Jason. "I'm going to go upstairs and check on Gemma."

She left the kitchen, and Jason remained standing in the doorway, his brows drawn together in confusion. "Why do I get the feeling I'm missing a big part of this conversation?" He hefted the bags and placed them on the countertop, his back to Ryder. "Anyway, I got some of those fish crackers Gem loves and some other stuff. I figured she'd want ice cr—"

"Jase. Can we sit for a minute?"

If only it were as simple as asking Jason for a hug and having it make it right. Ryder knew to choose his words carefully, in hopes of staving off the inevitable argument.

"Sure. What's up? Where were you this morning?" He took off his jacket and slung it over the back of his chair.

Forcing himself to sound as nonchalant as possible, Ryder said, "I, um, went to see my mother." His lips felt strangely stiff forming the words.

Jason stared back at him woodenly. "What are you talking about? We decided last night you wouldn't see her."

Praying his voice didn't shake, Ryder rubbed his hands together nervously, then laced his fingers together. "No, *you* decided. Like you always do whenever the conversation revolves around my mother or, frankly, my family."

"What the hell are you talking about?"

"You're always making the decisions in this marriage, Jase; from vacations to spending every Sunday night at your parents', and even whether or not I should see my mother. I've given in to you because it's easier than arguing. But now it not only involves me, it's Gemma's life. And like it or not, my mother is her grandmother, and after you told me she came by to see Gemma, I wanted to make one last-ditch effort to see if there was a relationship worth salvaging."

"I didn't know you resented me so much. You make me sound like a horrible person; like I always force you to do things against your will."

"That's not what—"

"You just said it. You give in because you don't want to fight with me. Like I'd never agree with you."

"Have you?" said Ryder, challenging him.

"I don't fucking believe this." With an angry shove to his chair, Jason stood and grabbed his jacket. "I thought when people loved each other they didn't keep secrets. I'm not even going to ask what else you're hiding from me." Without bothering to put the rest of the groceries away, he walked out of the kitchen.

Dumbfounded that Jason walked out on him, Ryder

scrambled after him. "What are you talking about? Secrets? I don't have any secrets from you. I told you everything." The front door slammed, and Ryder heard the sound of Jason's truck starting.

"Jason," he called out. "Jase. Come back."

But by the time he'd wrenched open the front door, all Ryder could see was the back of the truck receding in the distance. *Fuck.*

"Ryder? Jason?"

Helen came running down the stairs, concern evident in her eyes. "What happened?"

"Exactly what I'd feared. I told him, he freaked out and this time I don't think he's going to forgive me so easily."

He closed the door behind him and wandered back into the house to collapse on the sofa. "Why did I do it when I knew she wouldn't care? Why did I make her more important than what my husband wanted? I'm such an idiot."

"I'm not the one you should be saying this to. Go find Jason and tell him."

It wouldn't be that simple. Knowing Jason, his temper was at full throttle right now. Best to let him stew a while and hopefully cool off a bit before attempting to talk. The problem was Ryder wasn't sure what to say no matter how long it took.

Chapter Thirteen

THE FIRST THING Jason did was turn on the radio as loud as he could to drown out the angry voices in his head. Appropriately, "Highway to Hell" came on, and Jason's lips curled in a fierce, humorless grin.

Fucking right.

Without any idea what to do, Jason found himself heading toward the one place people never disappointed or judged him. He pulled into a parking space across from Drummers and hoped his friend John, who owned the bar, was there and not too busy to talk. Years ago, when Jason had a crisis of confidence in his relationship with Ryder, he came to speak to his friend, whose calm and practical nature helped talk Jason back off the ledge of cutting and running out on him.

This is different, thought Jason, as he walked in and sighed with relief at the sight of John behind the bar.

"Hey, Jase."

Abandoning his usual composure, John came out from behind the bar to give him a hug.

"I'm so glad Gemma's getting better. Liam was here

over the weekend and said she's been doing much better since you brought her home."

"Yeah. I'm almost afraid to say anything in case I jinx it, you know?" He laughed weakly, unwilling to let go of John. He wanted to stay here with his friend in this circle of understanding.

"Come on, let's sit down."

He followed John to a table. So many memories lived here; it was where he and Ryder fell in love and their relationship took root. His whole life changed within these walls; now it all seemed to be falling apart, and Jason had no idea what had happened and how to put it back together or even if he could. He began to shake.

"What's wrong? You look like you've lost your best friend." John gave him a sharp once-over. "Hold on, I'll be right back." He jumped up from his chair, but Jason barely paid attention, staring miserably at the television without seeing a thing. John returned only a few minutes later with two pints of beer. "Here. You look like you need this."

"Thanks." Jason took the glass but didn't drink the beer and instead stared into its foamy depths.

"Jason, what's wrong?"

"I—I feel like Ryder and I are headed for a breakup." His stomach turned over at those words, and he tasted acid in the back of his throat.

"The fuck you say."

He jerked his head up to stare at John, who rarely

cursed. The last time, Jason recalled, was when John called Liam out for not supporting Jason when he came out as bisexual.

"This past year's been so hard. I've worked my ass off with the business to not have to touch his trust fund or any money from his family, and that took time away from Gemma and him. Then when she got sick, our whole life got thrown out of whack, and we've barely spent any time together."

"But she's home. And she's gonna get better. Now you have the time to come back to each other."

"It's not that simple."

"Sure it is," said John, leaning forward with urgency. "It's simple unless you make it fucking difficult. You love each other. Goddamn it, I've never seen two people more perfect for each other, other than Connor and Emily. Don't make this anything bigger than it is."

"I haven't told you everything."

They eyed each other across the table, and his face pale, John hitched his chair closer. "He didn't cheat on you, or you on him, right?"

Horrified, Jason shook his head vehemently. "Of course not."

"Then fuck it. Nothing else matters."

"You don't understand. It's a matter of trust. Ryder did things without telling me, and I don't know if I can forgive him. He doesn't talk to me; he goes out and does what he wants even after we've discussed it and I thought we were good. How many times can I say I'm not hurt when I am? It's breaking me, and I'm so fucking close to coming apart for good."

"Jase, man, you don't throw it all away because you get butt-hurt over things. You talk and work things out. You have a life together. You have a child, for Christ's sake."

And sometimes a crisis allows a crack, not visible to the naked eye, to rise to the surface and cause a divide in a previously unblemished surface. Lucky were the ones who caught it early before it fractured, shattering into a mosaic of tears. Was it too late for him and Ryder?

"You need to—"

"Excuse me."

A man stood by their table, a large black shepherd dog by his side.

"I'm sorry, but you can't bring a dog in here." John gave him a half smile. "Board of Health regulations."

In need of a shave and a haircut, the man gave them both a weary grin. "I just got off the plane from Dubai. I've flown fourteen hours with Duffy here, who had it even worse than me. I'm hoping you can help me."

Jason eyed the dog, who sat quietly, tongue lolling out of his mouth. "He's a beauty."

"Thanks. He was in Afghanistan with us. I was discharged, and I couldn't leave him behind. Duffy's a certified therapy dog now."

Noticing John had gone still, Jason held out his hand. "Thank you for your service. John here is the owner of this place. I'm Jason Mallory."

"Nice to meet you. I'm Craig Whitmore." He turned to face John. "Are you John Drummer, Eric's brother?"

Jason's breath caught in his throat. *Shit.* This guy knew John's brother.

"Yes." John's voice came out no louder than a whisper.

A full-fledged smile broke out over Craig's face. Tiny lines fanned out over his tanned skin from the corners of his eyes. "Eric was my best friend. And Duffy here was his dog. They were inseparable. Duffy also took a bullet when your brother was killed by the sniper fire. He almost died." He stroked the dog's head, and the dog licked his hand. "You're a good boy, Duffy." The dog whined and pressed up against his legs.

Jason thought of Pearl and Trouper and missed their solid comfort and unconditional love.

"I have to go. Take my seat, Craig. It was nice meeting you. John, I'll call you."

"Jase, wait." A note of desperation crept into John's voice. "We didn't finish our talk."

"It's fine. I know what I have to do." Not really, but he wanted to leave the former soldier alone with John. Something about this man made Jason think he'd be important in John's life.

He headed out of the bar and into his truck. Before he started the engine he checked his messages and saw half a dozen missed texts from Ryder. He tapped out a quick answer.

Need time to think. Alone. TTYL.

He started the truck and began the trek back to downtown Brooklyn. Familiar with the shortcuts, he pulled up in front of Connor and Emily's brownstone, not even fifteen minutes later. The moment he rang the bell, Jason heard the barking of their two pit bulls, Laurel and Hardy. Better than any alarm system.

The door opened to Connor holding his daughter, Isabel. "Jase, what's up? Something wrong?" Alarm flared in his eyes. "Gem okay? Where's Ryder?"

"Whoa, hold up. Gem's fine; she's home with my mom and Ryder, taking a nap. I needed to talk, but if it's a bad time…" He gestured to little Isabel, who lay snuggled in Connor's arm, half asleep.

"Nah, come on in. Em and I were putting her down for a nap, but she's so zonked it'll only take a minute." He turned, and Jason followed him inside their cozy home. The dogs galloped up to Jason, whining their greeting, their tails furiously whipping back and forth. With his one free hand, Connor pointed to the sofa. "Hang out and I'll be right back."

With the dogs surrounding him, Jason relaxed on the sofa, and true to his word Connor returned in less than five minutes with Emily beside him.

"Jase, oh my God, I feel like we haven't seen you guys in forever. Now that Gemma's home we have to have a get-together." Emily kissed his cheek hello. "When she's able, of course," Emily added hastily, sitting across from him, cross-legged on the loveseat.

Laurel sat at her side, and Emily absently stroked the dog's head, fondling her silky ears.

This house had been as much a home to him as his own during the time he and Ryder dated and after their marriage. The happy memories surrounded him: dinners in Emily's huge kitchen, Sunday brunches out on the deck with the dogs and kids running around in the yard. Connor and Emily had become friends to him as much as they were to Ryder, and he valued their opinion.

"What's wrong?" Connor's sharp green gaze raked over him, and Jason shifted in his seat. "You look like shit." Ryder had always professed that Connor could pick up on bullshit right away, so Jason knew better than to prevaricate and fake an answer.

"Ryder and I are having problems. You've known him the longest and are his closest friends, so I thought maybe you could help me." He sought out Emily's sympathetic face. "I don't want to lose him."

Emily came to sit next to him and gave him a hug. "We are, but we're also your friends. I'm sure the strain of an illness like Gemma's would take a toll on anyone's relationship."

"Did something specific happen?" asked Connor. "I talked to Ry yesterday, and he sounded perfectly fine."

"We'd grown a bit distant even before Gem got sick. I was busy working late on-site, and he resented it, telling me I didn't need to, that we could use his grandmother's trust fund. But I didn't want that. I don't want anything from his mother."

"Okay. There has to be something more, Jase. I'm sure you'll be working less now that Gemma's home. Come on."

"Every time he's gone to see his mother, first to ask her to donate her bone marrow and then now, this morning, he never wants me there. I offered to support him and to show his mother that we're in love and strong and happy. But instead, he chose to go with his father and brother the first time, without any discussion, and today he went to see her again to talk to her, without even telling me."

"What about?" Connor frowned and folded his arms. "He didn't mention anything to me when I spoke to him last night."

"After the transplant I found her hanging outside Gemma's room and told her in no uncertain terms if she wanted to see Gemma, she had to accept me and our marriage. She made some bizarre comments, and when I told Ryder last night, I thought he agreed with me."

"Wait." Emily sounded confused. "That was over a month ago. You didn't tell him until now?"

"Well, yeah," admitted Jason. "But not deliberately. Only because I honestly forgot with everything else going on. His mother was not my top priority; Gemma was."

"Okay, so what happened next?"

Connor, Jason could tell, was very much in lawyer mode, taking in the facts and asking questions to the point.

"This morning everything was fine. He'd left early, but I thought it was to check on stuff he had to do in the office that couldn't wait. Instead I come home to find him sitting and talking with my mother, and it turns out he saw his mother again. This time he didn't even bother to tell me ahead of time that he planned to see her. He says I'm a distraction and he wants his mother to concentrate on the issues, not how much she hates me." The pain in his heart escalated until he found it hard to breathe, and Jason wondered if that was what a broken heart felt like.

"So what did you say?" Emily tucked her feet underneath her and rested her chin on her hands. "I can't imagine Ryder dismissed you without even listening to you."

"He accused me of steamrolling him every time we do something so that I get my way. I asked him what other secrets he's keeping from me, then walked out and went to Drummers, spoke to John, and then came here."

"Whoa. Wait." Connor's face scrunched up, a picture of confusion. "You don't talk about it with your husband but run out and talk to strangers? I mean, much as we love you guys, we're not in your bedroom or your life."

"I—I know you think I'm crazy, but Ryder's—"

"Nope." Connor held up his hand. "Stop. Ryder's been my best friend for almost fifteen years. And I love you too, man. This isn't right. Don't ask me to talk about my friend. The two of you need to sit down together and work through it. Not the four of us."

"I'm afraid."

Emily took his hand, but he barely noticed. He'd never felt so cold and alone. "It's like he doesn't need me anymore."

"Talk to him," said Connor. "Nothing worthwhile is easy. You think me and Emily always had it easy? No fucking way." He gave Emily a crooked smile. "It's damn hard to mesh your life with someone else's, but the payoff is worth everything. Right, baby?"

Emily got up from sitting next to him to slip her arms around Connor's neck and lay her cheek against his. "More than everything. Go to Ryder, Jase. It's easy to lose your way sometimes, but I have every faith you and Ryder will find your way back to each other. You love each other as much as Connor and I do. Talk it out."

What could he say? That in their years together he'd come to enjoy Ryder leaning on him and even encouraged it? Or that maybe he took advantage of Ryder's dislike of confrontation to always push his way forward? It didn't make him a bad person….Did it?

"You're right. I'm sorry I tried to drag you guys in the middle of our problems. It wasn't fair of me."

"It's okay." Emily left Connor's side to give him a hug. "I love that you trust us and feel so close to us that you did come. But I think you know what you have to do."

He met their gazes steadily.

"Yeah. I know where I'm going."

Chapter Fourteen

HOPEFUL THAT JASON would be on the same wavelength, Ryder turned the key in the lock to his in-laws' house and heard the warning barks from inside. He opened the door, but his heart sank at the empty house. He'd believed after he gave Jason some time to think, he might come here. Maybe they weren't as in tune as he'd thought.

"Hold up, you two. It's me."

Delighted yelps and barks burst from both Trouper and Pearl as they raced toward him from the back of the house, and Ryder sank down on the rug in the front hall. The two dogs swarmed over him, licking and pawing at him, and a wave of guilt washed over Ryder.

"We've really neglected you. I'm so sorry. I promise you'll be coming home soon."

Both Pearl and Trouper sat on their haunches, tongues lolling, intelligent brown eyes bright. He hugged each one tight, murmuring soothing words of praise and love.

Pearl lay across his lap, and Troup snuggled by his

side. Ryder bent down to lay his cheek against Pearl's neck. How many hours had he spent doing this before he met Jason, holding his dog for security and comfort?

Footsteps sounded on the porch, and his heart began to slam in heavy, painful beats when he heard the key jingling in the lock. The dogs jumped up again, barking their heads off. The front door opened, and an exhausted Jason walked in. He petted the dogs but never took his wary eyes off Ryder. It broke Ryder's heart to see his fun-loving husband so hesitant and sad. All he wanted to do was press reset to last year when they were untouched by any ugliness and pain.

"I was hoping to find you here."

It took everything he had not to pull Jason to him and say nothing mattered but their love, their history, and everything they'd shared together, but they needed to talk. Ryder stood, shushing the excited dogs, who couldn't stop jumping on them both. "You were? For what?"

Jason unzipped his jacket and tossed it on the decorative chair Helen had sitting by the entrance. "Don't tell my mother I did that. When we were kids she always yelled at me for throwing my jacket on that chair." His slight grin faded. "Can we go sit in the kitchen? My father keeps the whiskey there, and I need a shot."

Ryder's heart sank. Jason never drank hard liquor. "Sure."

He followed behind and sat down at the battered

table Helen said every year at Christmastime she couldn't bear to get rid of. The two dogs crowded by his legs, their tags jingling in the silence, and Ryder placed his hand on Pearl's neck, needing her warmth. He watched Jason slosh a little of his father's whiskey in a glass and drink it down with a shudder, then turn to face him, his face oddly strained and pale.

"On the outside we have the perfect life, you know? But inside I guess it wasn't so perfect. And maybe we both knew it and chose to ignore it because it's easier than dealing with hard truths about ourselves."

When had everything changed? From the very first, Jason had touched him like no one else, and Ryder could never imagine being with another man. But real life couldn't exist on a diet of happily ever afters. Every day presented a new struggle that if you chose to ignore, reached deep past the flawless exterior to chip away at the beauty inside.

"I love you, Jason. That hasn't changed, though."

The dogs, perhaps sensing his upset, whined and stood between them staring first at him, then at Jason. Innately intuitive, Pearl pressed against his legs and licked his hand, while Trouper jumped up on Jason, who gave him scratches behind the ears before pushing him down.

"And I love you more today than I did that night I came out to my parents. I could never stop loving you."

Ryder's heart began to bang in hard, painful thumps. "Why does this sound like there's a big 'but' coming?"

"Because," said Jason, joining him at the table and sitting across from him, "love isn't always enough. We've turned into strangers, Ry. Before Gem got sick I was working so late I barely remembered my own name at night before falling asleep. We hardly spent any time together; you know that."

"I know. And I said you didn't need to do that. But," Ryder hastened to add, "I understood why you thought you had to even though I didn't agree with it."

"And," said Jason, staring into his glass, "once she got sick, it got worse. I get that we were operating on fumes, where everything aside from her health fell by the wayside. But it's more than that. The 'us' part of our family fell apart as well."

Even though Ryder had a pretty good idea what Jason was going to say, he still wanted to hear it himself. "Tell me what you're thinking. Talk to me now."

He watched Jason's long fingers fidget, then grasp the glass of whiskey tight. "You've changed. You've made your mother the third person in our relationship. I know I've been hard on you when it comes to you and her, but I did it to protect you because I knew she'd end up rejecting you."

That admission surprised Ryder. "Protect me? I'm not a child who needs protection."

"I know, but you've been hurt so much by her. I couldn't stand seeing you waste your time on someone who didn't care. It reminded me of when we first met and no matter what you did, she turned her back on you. I didn't want you going back to thinking her behavior was somehow your fault."

"I don't think that. My mother has problems, but I'm not one of them."

"And then," Jason continued, "you kept leaving me out of all these important decisions. Even if you didn't want me there, I thought we'd agreed you'd tell me what you planned."

What Jason said was true. He had promised not to speak to his mother about Gemma without first discussing it, and he'd ignored Jason's feelings.

"You're right and I'm sorry. I thought it would end up less confrontational if I went myself."

Jason's face hardened. "Why do you make me out to be the bad guy? I wouldn't say anything to embarrass you if that's what you're worried about."

"Don't be ridiculous. But come on." Ryder hitched his chair close to the table and closer to Jason so their knees touched. "That's not what's really bothering you, is it?"

"What do you mean?"

This house had always been a place where Ryder felt welcomed and loved. He'd found his family here. But loving Jason and his family didn't negate his longing to find closure with his mother, no matter how dysfunctional their relationship was. And over the years they'd swept it under the rug; as if it hadn't been necessary to mention.

"I think you enjoyed me relying on you a little too much. You know how I hate confrontation and that I'd usually give in rather than argue a point."

"I didn't mean to."

"Yeah, you did, but I'm not blaming you. It was as much my fault as yours. I let you do it. Maybe it's because I never had anyone to rely on and trust, who loved me like you did, and I was afraid you would disappear. That if I pushed too hard or too often you'd get sick of it and me and leave."

Jason's astonished look would've been amusing if the conversation wasn't so serious. "I'd never do that, Ry. Do you really think I could leave you? Do you think so little of me?"

"No," said Ryder with a sad smile. "Not you. It's me. I guess I'm not as secure as I thought I was. Something else I need to work on." Frustrated, Ryder drummed his fingers on the table. "Look, I know I chose to live like this. But I'm not taking all the blame. Do you remember the last time I pushed you on anything?"

Moments passed, and Jason shook his head with a frown. "I can't, but that doesn't mean—"

"Jase. You don't understand. I'm not blaming you. It's as much my fault for allowing it to happen as it is yours for doing it. The last time I really pushed you was when you disappeared after the first time we made love; when I came inside you. Remember?"

At Jason's nod, Ryder slid his palm over Jason's

hand. "I tried again, before Gemma got sick, when I wanted us to go away for the weekend, but you insisted we stay here because you wanted to. I gave in, like I always did, because I think I made making you happy more important than making myself happy. And that's wrong."

"The two of us are both important. And I'm sorry I keep making comments about your mother."

"The negative comments about my mother stopped bothering me because deep down I knew she wouldn't come around and I didn't want the conflict. But now, inadvertently, she's been pushed back into our lives, and I can't ignore her anymore."

"And I didn't give you any slack, did I?" With a hesitancy that cracked Ryder's heart, Jason touched his hand, his red-rimmed eyes dark and weary.

The unexpected honesty from Jason gave Ryder hope they hadn't veered too far off course, and though the waters might be choppy, they'd stay together and come out on the other side of the storm stronger than before, with a better understanding of themselves as husbands and partners in life. Ryder squeezed Jason's hand tight.

"No, you didn't, so I figured why even bother to tell you anything when I knew what your answer would be? But it was wrong of me, and I'm sorry."

"I'm sorry too. It wasn't deliberate, like I meant it's my way or nothing. But I see now how it looked like that to you. I hated how much she hurt you and how you still kept going back, hoping for crumbs, when you deserve the whole fucking bakery, Ry. You deserve the world."

"I'd settle for a slice. But right now this isn't about her; we can get back to that. Going forward, I have to feel that my opinion is as valid as yours and that even if you disagree or want something else, you'll listen to me. I don't feel like that now. I may be a great negotiator in court and persuasive, but it's not personal to me."

Jason's brow furrowed. "I don't get it."

Frustrated he wasn't expressing himself as well as he could, Ryder took a deep breath and began again. "When I'm in court, I'm paid to argue for who I'm representing. I'm not personally invested in the outcome. I want to do the right thing, of course, but my heart isn't involved. But when it comes to us and our life, because I care about you I'm always willing to give in if I think it will make you happy."

"Is that what you do, give in to me whether you agree or not?"

"It's you I love. Everything you want matters to me." He laced their fingers together. "You and Gemma matter the most. Always."

"I feel the same. God, I was sick all day running around thinking I'd lost you, and nothing looked the same anymore: Drummers, Emily and Connor's house. Everywhere I looked, all I saw was us. You're part of me, Ry. Nothing can change that. I only knew what love wasn't before I met you. Once I met you, nothing else mattered but us."

"You went to those places?"

Jason nodded. "I needed perspective, and they all gave it to me in spades."

"Oh yeah?" Curious as to what their friends said to Jason, he prodded Jason with his foot. "What did they say?"

"That I shouldn't have run away. I needed to talk to you, not them. And they were right. I made the same mistake now that I made before we got married by running away instead of talking things out. I'm sorry it had to come to this."

"Maybe not, if it can turn a negative into a positive for us." Touched and relieved, Ryder stood and pulled Jason up with him. "Are we good now? We know what we have to do, right?"

A wicked gleam brightened Jason's eyes, and a corresponding wave of desire washed over Ryder. "I wasn't talking about that. I meant going forward we have to talk out both our sides and not dismiss each other's feelings, right?"

"Yeah." Jason kissed his neck. "I'm going to be more considerate, I promise. I won't ever steamroll you again. But you gotta let me know if I fuck up. Okay? I yell orders at guys all day long; I'm used to being in charge."

Ryder leaned his forehead against Jason's, falling into his wonderful, familiar scent, molding himself against the body he'd come to know as well as his own. Thank God. They were going to come out of this even stronger than before. For the first time in a long time, Ryder felt he and Jason were walking side by side in their relationship on equal footing.

"I like you being in charge sometimes. It has its benefits." Ryder slipped his arms around Jason's neck. "You can be in control in the bedroom anytime you like."

"How about the kitchen?" Jason pushed him up against the counter, and a delicious ache rolled through him as Jason's hot mouth trailed kisses down his neck while his hand snaked down the front of his jeans to pop open the button and yank down the zipper. "I want you. Right here. Your dick in my mouth."

Those erotic words, coupled with the brush of Jason's lips against his, spiked a hunger almost forgotten these past months, and Ryder hurriedly pushed his jeans and boxers down over his hips until they sagged to his ankles. He wouldn't last long, he knew, not with the way Jason eyed him, like a lion heading in for the kill. The beginning tingles of his orgasm fluttered at the base of his spine, and he moaned at the first touch of Jason's mouth on his cock.

"Fuuuck." He scrabbled with his hand to find purchase against the countertop and bucked his hips.

But apparently Jason didn't plan on a quickie. He nuzzled into Ryder's stomach, skimming his fingers lightly over Ryder's hips, flicking his tongue first into Ryder's belly button, then over his balls, licking them, then sucking each one into his mouth. Jason loved giving head, and Ryder loved nothing more than the sight of his husband between his legs. Then he forgot everything when Jason's hot, wet mouth slid down his cock.

The pressure built, traveling up his spine, electrifying his nerves, and finally splintering him apart from the force of the orgasm crashing through him. The absolute abandon of making love, unclouded now by the weight of Gemma's illness, feeling the silk of Jason's hair sliding through the clutch of his fingers, the bite of Jason's fingers into his naked skin, and the wet heat of his loving mouth and tongue bonded him and Jason tighter. Forever, never to be broken.

"Oh God," Ryder cried out as he shook and climaxed. He closed his eyes and dragged in deep breaths. After a moment he opened his eyes and smiled down at Jason. "I love you. I promise never to keep you in the dark again." He held out a hand to Jason to help him up. "And I promise to take care of you later. But first, let's talk. Everything out in the open, right?"

Jason gave him a warm smile, then kissed him, and Ryder tasted himself on Jason's lips. "I love you too, babe." Before Ryder could speak further, Jason bent down and pulled his jeans and boxers up, and Ryder zipped up and buttoned them. "Let's go into the other room and sit." With their arms around each other's waists, they walked into the living room. The dogs, who had been lying down in the hallway, jumped up and followed them, nails clicking on the hardwood floors.

He took a spot on the wide leather sofa and stretched out. "Come." Ryder patted his lap, sighing with pleasure when Jason crowded up next to him, pillowing his head in his lap. "I missed this alone time."

"Yeah, me too." Jason yawned, the words rumbling in his chest. "So. You went to talk to your mother."

So much else had happened it felt like years passed since this morning instead of mere hours. "Yeah. And it wasn't pretty." He showed the pen he'd found in his mother's apartment to Jason then relayed the conversations with both Emmaline and his mother. Jason's body tensed as he spoke. When he finished, he buried his lips in Jason's dark waves and murmured, "What do you think?"

"I think," said Jason, raising his head to lock eyes with Ryder, "maybe we need to pay a visit to the mysterious Emmaline."

Chapter Fifteen

"MOM, HOW'S GEMMA? Can we impose on you and Dad a little more? Ryder and I have to go someplace." He winked at Ryder, who sat on the floor, scratching Pearl's belly. "Good. Don't let her do too much. She may say she's feeling better, but she still needs to take it easy. We'll be back as soon as we can."

With the phone tucked under his ear, Jason joined Ryder on the floor, rubbing his bare feet over Ryder's. He leaned over and kissed his shoulder. Now that they'd cleared the air, the horrible pain he'd been carrying around inside him had vanished. Jason could breathe again, and it felt damn good.

"Yes, he's here with me." At Ryder's laugh, he rolled his eyes. "Yes, Mom. Everything is fine. We talked it out, and it's all good. Oh, by the way, we're at your house, visiting the pups, and then we're gonna make a stop, then come home. Look, I gotta go. Love you, bye." He clicked off and tossed the phone on the sofa. "Jesus, it was like being questioned by the FBI—'What happened, is everything okay, did you and Ryder work it out?' " He caught Ryder's eyes, and they burst out laughing and didn't stop until their eyes teared and they couldn't catch their breath.

"Yeah, I'd say we worked it out. If your mother only knew how you accosted me in the kitchen." Ryder snickered and wiped his eyes.

"Please," said Jason, jumping to his feet and stretching out the kinks in his back. "I could tell you stories of the girls Liam used to sneak into the basement or the parties we had here when we were teenagers."

"Do you ever miss it? Being with a woman, I mean."

Shocked at the question, Jason stood speechless in the center of the room. From the first time he'd kissed Ryder, the thought of being with anyone else had never crossed his mind.

"Are you serious?"

"In a curious way. Not in an 'I think you're sorry you're with me' way." Ryder collected his socks and pulled them on. "I'm not worried you're going to leave me for a woman."

"Or a man. Of course I still notice women. I'm not dead. Like I'm sure you admire beautiful men. But admiration doesn't mean anything. It's you I love and want in my life."

"I know." Ryder looked up at him from under the fall of his hair with a smirk. "I'm picturing you and Liam sneaking girls into the house as teenagers."

"I've graduated to sneaking my husband in and jumping him any chance I get." To prove his point,

Jason tackled Ryder to the sofa, kissing him until Ryder gasped for breath and moaned against his lips.

"Jase, we can't."

"Why not?" He couldn't help his petulant tone. The unmistakable bulge of Ryder's erection prodded his thigh. Jason studied his face as he reached up to sweep Ryder's hair away from his face and kept his hand threaded in the thick silk. He never got tired of touching Ryder or looking at him. "I want you."

A teasing light entered Ryder's eyes. " 'Cause I can't have sex with you in every room of this house. I'd never be able to look your mother in the eye again." He sobered up. "Plus, we have to go into the city, and we don't want to get stuck in rush-hour traffic. That'll make a tense situation even worse."

Desire drained out of him at the thought of what lay ahead. "Yeah, you're right," he said, yet he kept his arms around Ryder. "I'm holding you to later tonight, though."

After a bit more kissing and nuzzling, Ryder sat back on his heels. "It's a date."

They sat up and returned to putting on their socks and sneakers. With regret, Jason looked down at the two dogs waiting all bright-eyed and hopeful at their feet.

"Damn. You guys, I'm sorry. I know you want to come home. Not yet. Maybe in a couple of weeks."

Ryder knelt and looped an arm around each dog's neck. "You two deserve a medal. It's been hell for you too, huh?" At his praise, they licked his face and wagged their tails. "Your little girl has to get stronger still. She can't wait to see you either."

And as if they understood, both Trouper and Pearl gave him a bark and went to Jason, who hugged them both. "Mom and Dad will be back later, and we'll come visit you tomorrow, okay?" With one last pat and scratch, he held out a hand to Ryder and pulled him up, not letting him go as the dogs danced around their feet. Jason pulled out his phone and for a few minutes took videos of them, knowing how much Gemma missed her doggies.

Ryder handed him his jacket and zipped up his own. "We'd better get going." The dogs had disappeared to the back of the house, and he and Ryder walked out, down the steps to the car waiting for them in front.

"I have my truck." He jerked a thumb to the driveway, where his truck sat parked.

"We can either pick it up later or tomorrow. The last thing I want is to have to concentrate on driving. It's going to be a zoo." Ryder opened the back door to the car, and Jason scrambled inside the hushed interior, Ryder sliding in next to him. He slammed the door shut, and the car took off.

"I could get used to this," said Jason with a sigh, relaxing against the soft leather seats.

"So you don't mind when my father gives us the use of his car, then?"

Jason turned his head to face an unsmiling Ryder.

"That's a loaded question."

Ryder quirked a brow. “Not really. You don’t want to accept the money from my grandmother’s trust fund to pay for the mortgage on the house or send Gemma to school because you see it as coming from my mother, yet you have no problem riding around in my father’s car.”

Jason opened his mouth to deny Ryder’s accusation but found himself unable to disprove what he’d said. *Shit.*

“Hmm.”

Ryder laughed and nudged his shoulder. “I recognize that ‘*hmm.*’ You know I’m right yet don’t want to admit it ’cause then you’d be wrong.”

Incapable of disagreeing, Jason gave a sheepish grin. “Guess you’re right. I didn’t see it that way until you just pointed it out.”

“Let’s leave that issue aside for now. What do you think our plan of action should be when we speak to Emmaline? I don’t want her to feel like she’s being attacked or interrogated, but between what she said and my mother’s outburst to me afterward, I think she knows stuff about my mother’s past and what made her the way she is.”

“Like what?” For Jason, it was obvious. Ryder’s mother was a homophobe and a snob who only cared about herself.

“I don’t know; that’s the frustrating part.” A frown creased his face. There was little Jason could do for him except show his support, so he took his hand and squeezed it tight.

"Whatever it is, I'm glad I'll be there with you."

At his words, Ryder's expression cleared. "Me too. Maybe I was wrong not to have brought you all along to show her what a strong marriage we have."

"Well, don't dwell on the past." They'd only gotten back on stable footing this afternoon, and Jason had no intention of sliding backward with recriminations and regret. "I'm here now. I'll always be right here at your side."

"Thanks, babe." Ryder leaned over and kissed him, his soft lips warm against Jason's, and as always when Ryder touched him, his body flamed. There could never be anyone else for him but this man, and he was so grateful to have the rest of his life to show him how much.

"Don't thank me. It's what you do for the person you love." He reached up and brushed back the silk of Ryder's hair. "I'm so damn glad I get to do it all with you."

They spent the rest of the ride in relative silence. The closer they got to the hotel, the more tense Ryder became until by the time the car pulled up in front of the St. Regis, he looked visibly ill.

"Babe, calm down. It's going to be fine." The hotel loomed in front of them in all its stately elegance. They exited the car, but Ryder held back, hesitating on the sidewalk, and Jason, who'd advanced a few steps ahead, turned around to face Ryder. "Ry, what's going on?

Why're you so freaked out?"

"I don't know."

"Let's go do this." Jason took Ryder's hand and passed through the gilt doors held open by the ornately liveried doorman. He stopped short, eyeing the grand lobby, the lavish furniture. "Whoa, this place is insane. I've never seen so much marble in my life." His architect's eye took in the soaring ceilings, decorative arches, and overall grandeur of the space. "It looks more like a museum than a hotel lobby."

Finally Ryder smiled. "I'm not surprised you think that. The hotel was built by the Astor family back in 1904 at the height of everything grand and glorious. They have some magnificent artwork we can take a look at before we leave. Salvador Dalí, his wife, and his pet ocelot used to live here."

"No kidding. That's cool."

"Yeah," said Ryder, seemingly more at ease now. "And the Bloody Mary was invented in the bar here. There's a lot of history in these walls."

Funny how you could live your whole life in a city and not know its history. "You're a regular walking history lesson. How do you know all this stuff?"

They approached the front desk, and Ryder shrugged. "My mother's side of the family is related to the Astors in some convoluted way. They're cousins a few times removed."

Holy shit. "Uh, what? The Astor Place Astors?"

Uncomfortable now, Ryder nodded. "Yeah, but we

don't ever see them except at weddings and funerals. That sort of thing."

Stunned, Jason struggled to recover from the bombshell Ryder so nonchalantly dropped in his lap. He'd always known Ryder's family had money but assumed it was the kind of wealth where you didn't have to think twice about buying something in a store or paying next month's mortgage. But this kind of money was a game-changer, something people only dream about or read in magazines. Those people were part of New York City history, famous in their own right. Now he understood. To cut Gemma off from Ryder's family deprived her of a heritage she had every right to belong to. Anything less would be selfish on his part.

"Good afternoon, gentlemen." The elegantly dressed concierge greeted them. "How may I be of service?"

Jason, still digesting what Ryder had told him only moments before, stayed silent, allowing Ryder to take the lead.

"Good afternoon. I was wondering if you could ring the room of Mrs. Emmaline Heaton and tell her Ryder Daniels is here to speak with her?"

Jason hadn't heard Ryder use that elegant, refined tone of voice in many years; he'd forgotten how sexy it sounded. It sure was a hell of a lot classier than the way he and Liam screamed at the guys working on the construction site.

"One moment, please, Mr. Daniels."

The concierge stepped to the side and placed a call,

keeping his voice discreetly low. He hung up after a few spoken words and returned to them.

"Mrs. Heaton stated you should come to her suite." He wrote the room number down and handed it to him on a card. "Mr. Iverson, her butler, will take you up to the Royal Suite. He'll be waiting for you by the elevator."

"Thank you," said Ryder. Jason gave a faint smile and trailed behind Ryder. *Royal suites, butlers, the Astor family.* All this tumbled through Jason's brain as they walked to the elevator. What did he have to offer a man like Ryder? A house in Brooklyn and movie night on a wide-screen television?

A beautifully dressed man stood waiting by the elevators.

"Mr. Daniels?"

"Yes. This is my husband, Jason Mallory."

"Pleasure to meet you, sir."

Once again, Jason found it hard to speak and merely nodded a greeting. Ryder, perhaps sensing his unease, stopped and motioned for Mr. Iverson to give them some privacy. The man withdrew discreetly.

"Hey, you. What's wrong?"

Ryder slid a warm palm up his cheek, but Jason averted his eyes. Maybe Ryder's mother was correct in that he didn't belong here.

"Don't," said Ryder sharply. "This is why I never speak of my family history or money. I could have all the money in the world, but without you, none of it matters. You and me and the life we've created together. Our beautiful, healthy daughter. That's what's real and important. The only thing that matters to me. Never second-guess yourself and what you mean to me."

All his misgivings melted away when he met Ryder's eyes and saw the fierce love brimming in their depths. They had a home—not merely a house—built on memories, laughter, and devotion. They'd created a family together. An unbreakable bond. But always most important, they had love. Love for each other and love for the life they created.

"I won't. As long as you're with me."

"Always, babe. That's a given."

Hand in hand they continued to the elevators where Iverson waited patiently. The butler held the elevator door for them, and they stepped into the cab. The ride took only a few moments, and Jason found himself following Iverson and Ryder down a hushed hallway, his footsteps sinking into plush carpeting. They stopped before a door that looked like it led into an apartment rather than a hotel room. Iverson rang the lighted bell inset in the solid wooden frame of the impressive-looking door. Soft chimes echoed faintly from within.

The door opened, and an elegant woman in her mid-to-late fifties stood before him. She might have been the same age as his mother, but her face bore barely a line or wrinkle. It spoke of hours spent at the spa or perhaps the hand of a plastic surgeon. Her gaze swept over them, dark and weary, as if whatever secrets she might be carrying had become too heavy to bear.

"Mrs. Heaton. Mr. Daniels and Mr. Mallory for you. May I bring you anything?"

"No, thank you."

"If you need anything, don't hesitate, please." He gave them an efficient nod and strode back down the hallway.

Emmaline Heaton held the door to her suite open wide. "Please come inside."

They walked into her opulent suite; large windows overlooked the city skyline. They stepped into a formal living room with a marble fireplace and sumptuous leather furniture. This might have been any luxury apartment in Manhattan; oil paintings adorned the silk-covered walls, and as they entered farther into the suite, Jason saw rooms branching out down the hallway and nudged Ryder. "This place is bigger than your old apartment. Somehow I don't picture anyone hanging out watching a football game on Sunday, huh?"

A brief smile flickered over Ryder's lips.

"Ryder? I'm surprised to see you." Emmaline spoke as she led them into the living room and indicated they should sit before the fireplace. They removed their jackets and sat next to each other on the sofa, holding hands, fingers laced together. "I'm glad you brought your husband to meet me." She addressed him with an encouraging smile. "I'm Emmaline; please don't call me Mrs. Heaton. Reminds me of my deceased mother-in-law, whom I had little fondness for, nor she for me."

"I'm Jason Mallory."

The charming smile lasted only a moment; then she turned back to Ryder. "While I am happy to see you again I must admit I'm curious. How did you find me?"

Ryder gave him an anxious glance, and he nodded with encouragement, giving Ryder's hand a gentle squeeze.

"After the aborted discussion with my mother, I found a St. Regis pen on the floor. I took a chance that it was yours, and here we are. Thank you for seeing us."

"And why was your talk with Astrid so brief?"

"I have no idea. I guess that's why we're here. I feel as though everyone is talking in circles around me and there's some big piece of the puzzle I'm not getting."

Emmaline turned her frank gaze on him, and Jason could see she was a woman who'd spent her life demanding respect and having her questions answered.

"What do you have to say about all this, Jason? As an outsider, I mean."

"Do you want my honest opinion?"

Her eyes warmed with good humor. "I expect nothing less, and I imagine you'll give it to me. You don't look like a man who holds back his emotions."

Ryder chuckled. "You've been pegged."

"I don't mind," said Jason with a grin of his own, which faded as he gathered his thoughts. "I don't think of myself as an outsider, though. I'm Ryder's husband and Gemma's father, so I do have a stake in this. But my main concern is Ryder. Whatever he wants to happen I stand by him one hundred percent."

"As a good husband should."

"I've never been given a chance by Ryder's mother to show her the type of person I am. She doesn't even know her own son and what a kind and decent human being he is. She tossed him out and gave up on him because he's gay? What kind of mother does that? She has no idea what our marriage is like or how much we love each other. All because she doesn't approve of same-sex marriage. It's not the 1950s." He let go of Ryder's hand to twist the heavy band of gold on his finger. "Then she makes remarks like 'It wasn't so easy for people back then' or 'We had to do what we were told.' I always believe if you have something to say, then spit it out. Stop talking in riddles."

"She told me she never wanted to get married or have children." Ryder's soft voice pierced Jason's heart. "That's hard for a child to hear from their parent."

"Oh, Ryder." Emmaline gazed at him with pity. "She didn't mean it that way."

"You think? The meaning was clear to me. I don't understand, though, why she bothered to get married in the first place."

"Family expectations," said Emmaline, sadly. "We had a lot of pressure on us back then. We did what we were told."

The laugh from Ryder sounded anything but cheerful. "That excuse only goes so far. And that's why we're here. You knew her when she was younger and a teenager. Maybe there's something you can tell us about why she seems on the brink of wanting to connect with our daughter yet still refuses to acknowledge not only our marriage but me as well."

Jason hated seeing Ryder so upset and rubbed his back, feeling his shirt damp with sweat, his body trembling.

Emmaline looked on with sympathy. "I'm sorry, Ryder. I know it must be hard for you."

"Hard? My mother wants nothing to do with me. How do you think that makes me feel?"

"I think we could use some tea." Emmaline pressed a buzzer on the phone and requested a tea tray. The understatement of the year. That must be what the very rich do to calm an unpleasant situation down. Jason wanted to correct her and tell her a bottle of vodka would be more like it. Maybe two.

Finished with her call, Emmaline sat quietly for a moment before speaking. "I've always believed it was your mother's story to tell and still do. Trust me when I say that you aren't the only one who's been hurt."

Exasperated with what he saw once again as people talking doublespeak around him, Jason narrowed his eyes, keeping a comforting arm around Ryder. "You know what? I don't really care if she was hurt years ago. Time to get over it for the good of her son and granddaughter. My God, how can anyone be so cold? She doesn't have to come for dinner every Sunday, but at least open the damn lines of communication, for

Christ's sake. Whatever it was couldn't be that bad. And even if it was, it's done and gone. Time to move on."

The doorbell rang as Emmaline drew a breath, poised to answer. "That'll be our tea," she said and got up to answer the door. She swung the door open wide. "Come in, please. You can set it down on the coffee table."

"Emmaline. Thank God you're here. I need you."

Beneath his arm, Ryder began to shake in earnest. "Mother? What are you doing here?"

Chapter Sixteen

IT MIGHT HAVE been a scene from a Fellini movie, Ryder thought. Here he sat with Jason, both of them in jeans and sweatshirts in a $6,500 per night luxury suite. Across from him sat his mother, pale yet determined-looking, the only sign of her obvious turmoil was her white-knuckled grip on her handbag. He half expected someone to jump out from behind the sofa or out of one of the rooms and yell, "Gotcha. It's all a dream."

But no such luck. The tea tray had arrived only minutes after his mother, and though Emmaline had poured out the smoky tea for all of them, only she had bothered to take a sip; his mother's, Jason's, and his cups were all left sitting on the silver tray to grow cold.

Before he could formulate the words running through his brain, Jason spoke up.

"Don't you think, Mrs. Daniels, that the time is way past due to put this one-sided argument to rest and make peace? I'm not asking to be your friend. Hell, you don't even have to pretend to like me. But for Ryder's sake and the sake of our daughter—your flesh and blood granddaughter—it's time to forgive and move on."

"That's a very pretty speech, Mr. Mallory."

"For God's sake, Mother. His name is Jason."

She tipped her head to him. "I know what his name is. I know everything about him. Did you think I'd let my granddaughter be raised by someone I didn't thoroughly check out first?"

"How dare you?" He half-rose in his seat, but Jason pulled him back down. "What did you hope to accomplish by doing that? Did you think you'd find some deep secret Jason's been keeping from me?" He slapped his hand on the sofa, aware of Emmaline's eyes on him. "What you want or think has no bearing on how we choose to live or raise Gemma. But she has a whole other side of family. Your side. They have no idea of her existence. And don't try and pull it over on me that it's because I'm gay that you're keeping us separate. Trust me, there are other gay members of your family."

"You have to know it's very in now to have gay friends, Mrs. Daniels. We're very sought after as party guests." Jason's attempt at humor fell flat.

"You think it's funny, don't you, *Jason*?" The emphasis couldn't be denied. "That it's something to make fun of because of everything that happened these past years. But some people never had that chance. They were forced to conform, sometimes with terrible consequences. You've been lucky to be able to live with the person you love most in the world. What if you couldn't? What if you were ripped apart and forced into a life you didn't want but had no alternative but to accept?"

Realization dawned as Ryder digested his mother's words. "Are you talking about yourself? You were in love with someone unacceptable to your family?"

His mother clutched her purse tighter and gave a tiny nod. "It was the 1970s, and we were teenagers. We spent every moment together, and it was wonderful. I'd finally understood what it meant to be loved and in love."

"It sounds beautiful."

"It does, doesn't it?" she said sadly. "But in reality we were fooling ourselves. There wasn't any future for us, and we knew it. But for a time we thought we'd captured the moon, and it was glorious."

The story sounded like a retelling of Romeo and Juliet or some other Shakespearian love tragedy.

"And then one night we found a way to be together, more intimately than we'd ever been before, and afterward we knew we'd never love anyone else the way we loved each other. We became inseparable for the entire year."

"What happened?" Did he die young? Certainly a horrible story but not one that should have caused her to turn against him and life in general.

"We were discovered. And to keep everyone's silence, we were separated. I was sent home, and my father watched me like a hawk. When I was twenty-one, he made sure I married the man he wanted."

His father. Ryder never bothered to ask how his parents met or fell in love. They'd always been an incongruous pair to him. Ryder barely felt Jason's arm around him as he listened to his mother's pathetic story. "So you never loved Dad?"

With no need to pretend any longer she shook her head, "No, I didn't love him; I couldn't. I was dead inside. It was years before I let him touch me."

"Look how many people you've hurt, how many lives you came close to ruining. You didn't want to have a relationship with me? Fine. But you actively tried to ruin my relationships with my father and my brother. What was the point in that?"

In the face of her continued silence, her unblinking gaze infuriated him.

"How can you live with yourself? I've never met anyone so cold." He slammed his hand down. "You can at least admit you were wrong. My God, Mother, I really think you are a monster."

She visibly flinched and he knew he'd struck home.

Good. Let her know the hurt I've felt all these years.

Was it his imagination or did he see a glimmer of regret in her eyes? "Your father didn't deserve to be duped. But it's too late for regret and recriminations. There's nothing I can do to change the past."

All the late hours and nights his father spent away from home now made sense to Ryder. He wondered if his father had ever loved his mother and tried to make the marriage work at first, or if he'd found someone else when he was pushed away so often he finally gave up. Ryder knew he could never ask.

"Well this is all a very sad story, but I don't get how any of it pertains to Jason and me and your unnatural hatred of our life." Knowing that she still refused to soften her stance toward him made it hard for Ryder to feel any sympathy. "I would think that because you were denied the love of your life, you'd want to see your children happy."

"How could it? Something died inside me when we were separated. I had nothing—no love, no hope, no choice. I'd been forced to live a fake life, and there you came, parading around with 'love is love' and everyone going out of their way to show their support. It didn't make me happy; it did the opposite. It embittered me and made me angry for everything I'd lost."

This whole conversation, like every other one he'd had with his mother, made him only more confused. "What do my sexuality and marriage have to do with you and the man you fell in love with?"

Jason nudged his elbow and whispered in his ear, "Ry, look." And it was then he noticed what he'd been blind to all along. His mother sitting next to Emmaline, their hands next to each other's on the loveseat, not touching yet touching. It couldn't be, but it was.

Emmaline? Was Emmaline the lover she talked about?

As if to confirm his thoughts, Emmaline picked up

his mother's hand and held it, gazing back at them defiantly. "We've waited over forty years to be able to be together. I told Astrid she should have told you long ago."

Holy shit. This could not be happening. Glancing over at Jason, Ryder knew his husband's shocked expression mirrored his own. His heart slammed in painful beats, and Ryder struggled for his breath and understanding.

"Wait, what? Mother? You were in love with Emmaline? This makes even less sense."

The strain in her white face proved it was no joke. "Not if you understood the pain I went through. I had to keep myself and my feelings hidden my whole life because I was born at the wrong time. Then you came, proudly declaring who you were and who you loved, and all I saw was my own wasted life."

One thing that hadn't changed was her ability to make everything about her. The story she'd told him was tragic, but no less than other older people who'd also been forced to live closeted lives. That still didn't explain her cruelty to him, Landon, and Jason.

"I'm sorry that you both didn't have the life you wanted. That you should have been able to have. But that doesn't excuse the horrible things you said to me: that I shouldn't have been born or that you wished I wasn't your son."

"Oh, Astrid, you didn't." Emmaline dropped his mother's hand, her expression a combination of horror, pity, and revulsion.

"She did. And don't think her behavior toward him hasn't screwed Ryder up in his personal life, before and after our marriage," Jason interjected, his voice thick with emotion. "She tried to ruin his relationship with his brother and father. Who could live like that and not be damaged?"

"I never should have had children. I may have done some things wrong and used a poor choice of words, but I'm not about to lie."

The gene responsible for warmth and kindness had certainly missed his mother, Ryder decided. Even now, with her greatest secret revealed, she remained as cold and blank as a marble statue.

"I don't understand you at all. I'm a parent now, and having Gemma and being her father is the greatest joy in my life."

The internal struggle showed on her face until finally, she set her purse down and clasped her shaking hands in her lap. "Everyone is different. Having children wasn't what I dreamed of. I wanted to live in Europe where alternative lifestyles were accepted. I wished to study art in a society I knew would understand me; I wanted to live free and unencumbered. But I couldn't. After we'd been caught, my father swooped in to do damage control. No one could find out; the scandal would be enormous. Emmaline's parents sent her abroad to finish her studies, and I came home to New York, and virtual house arrest, where my parents planned out every move I made."

"Like you did with Landon." In high school his brother had been forced to give their mother an itinerary of where he went and who with. Only Jason's quick thinking had allowed the two of them to see each other on the sly.

"I suppose I did," she admitted. "And then to find out you were gay was like the ultimate cruel joke. After everything I'd gone through, the irony of me having two boys, one of whom was gay, wasn't lost on me. I kept my distance from you because it hurt too much. But you kept pushing to see Landon and your father and me. Pushing for acceptance, pushing for more. More from me than I could give. I couldn't have you bring your lovers into my house, reminding me every day of what I could have had."

The earlier pity Ryder felt for his mother vanished, replaced by anger at her selfishness.

"You made everything about you when it should have been about your children and your family. And the worst part is you still don't see it. In all my life I've never known a more vain, self-centered person than you, Mother." All the old pain and humiliation he'd buried for decades, the desperate attempts to make her love him, to make himself more lovable, bubbled to the surface, wiping out the carefully placed shield of indifference he wore. "I can't even imagine how you got pregnant or why."

"I had no intention of doing so," she blurted out.

"Your father and I didn't consummate our marriage until years had passed. I told him on our wedding night I would never have sex with him and I didn't mind him going outside our marriage to get what he needed."

He didn't want to know but had to ask. "What happened to make you change your mind?"

"I did," said Emmaline. "Several years later I called your mother to tell her I got married, but that I still loved her. My husband wasn't as kind a man as your father. He raped me on our wedding night." Dark eyes, black as the night, held his. "I bought a gun after that, and the next time he came to me I told him if he touched me again, I'd shoot him." She smiled thinly. "He took the hint and never bothered me again."

The gilded walls of the rich held so many secrets. Money didn't solve problems; it created a new and different set, some with unintended consequences that left collateral damage like him, his brother, father, and even his mother as victims. And Emmaline, who suffered alone, in her courage found a strength she didn't know she possessed.

"I'm so sorry."

The corner of her mouth tipped up in a smile. "I'm not. I longed for that bastard to give me an excuse to shoot him."

"I still don't understand," he said, returning to question his mother, who fumbled in her purse for a tissue. "You can't make me believe Dad attacked you."

"No," she said after wiping her wet eyes. "After I

hung up with Emmaline, I wandered down to the library and proceeded to get a little drunk. Your father found me crying on the sofa. He picked me up and brought me to my room, and I held on to him." Lost in her memories, her eyes took on an unfocused look. "I was so lonely for her, but she wasn't there and he was. He held me and was so warm. I'm ashamed to say I used him as a stand-in. My only justification was the hope that maybe I'd finally feel something instead of being numb all the time."

Ironically, to Ryder this made more sense than anything else she could have said.

"But of course nothing had changed." Her eyes remained riveted to the floor. "Except six weeks later I discovered I was pregnant. Your father of course was overjoyed, but I only saw it as another means of binding me to something and someone I didn't want."

"I'm surprised you went through with the pregnancy," said Ryder, unable to keep the rancor out of his voice.

She raised her gaze from the floor. "I almost didn't. I told Emmaline I wanted to get an abortion, but she talked me out of it. She said it would be too dangerous."

Ryder's heart hurt from the pain of her words. "Perhaps Emmaline should have raised me, not you," he said bitterly. "She's had more feelings for me even before I was born than you've ever had."

"I'm giving you what you asked for: the truth. Some people aren't made to be parents. I'm one of them."

"Wait. I'm confused. How did you have Landon, then? You can't tell me you got drunk again ten years later."

"No, of course not." Unwilling to face him, she sat in profile, like that bloodless statue. "I'd received word that my mother had passed away. With both my parents gone, I realized I'd led a wasted life. I had nothing and nobody to love."

"You had me," said Ryder softly. Jason's hand crept into his, warm and life-giving.

"No." She shook her head. "I couldn't give you love. Not you, or anyone. I had nothing left inside. I was empty, nothing but a shell. Yet your father came to me and begged me to have another child. He thought maybe it would help spark something between us, and he didn't want you to grow up alone."

"I'm glad someone cared enough." Not having Landon would have made his life unbearable.

"I agreed, but only on the condition that you went away to boarding school. I knew I couldn't handle two children at once. Not when I hadn't planned on having any."

This long-sought truth failed to give him the satisfaction he'd hoped, and Ryder now realized Jason might have been correct all along. The past might have been better off left undisturbed, like a path of freshly fallen snow. Pure and clean.

"I'd say thank you for being honest, but I don't think I can. It's too late for that now. I don't give a damn anymore." Having finally got the answer to his life-long question about why he never measured up, Ryder saw no purpose in staying any further. Let his mother and Emmaline catch up on their lives and maybe find some happiness. Gemma waited for them at home. That's where he belonged. He stood and picked up his jacket. And as Ryder knew he would, Jason stood with him at his side like he had from the beginning.

"I'm not looking for you to accept Jason. We love each other, with or without your approval." Once again, Jason took his hand, his strength and love flowing into Ryder, warming him. "I can't force you to have maternal feelings for Landon or me; that's something lacking inside you. I'm sorry you were hurt and unable to live your life how you should have been, but cutting yourself off emotionally from us seems pointless now. You only get one chance to live your life; why do it with regrets?"

With their hands still clasped firmly, he and Jason walked to the door, but not before he stopped and turned around to face his mother, still sitting stiff and straight. Perhaps it would be the last time he'd ever see her unless she changed. "I've been stupid to keep Gemma away from your side of the family, thinking I needed your approval. I don't. She deserves to know her cousins and have her whole family around her, not just Jason's family and Dad's. It's the twenty-first century, Mother. Less and less people care who anyone sleeps with, and if they do, I don't need them in my life."

Pausing only to catch his breath, he tipped his head to Emmaline. "Thank you for seeing us. It was nice to talk with you."

"I wish both of you only the best, and for your little girl. If you find it possible, please try to keep in touch."

The late afternoon sunlight, diffused by the sheer curtains covering the windows, played across Emmaline and his mother. Perhaps they'd find a way to be together now and see if their almost half-a-century-old love stood the test of time.

"How odd, isn't it, that a virtual stranger wishes me the best, yet the woman who carried me and gave birth to me still can barely stand to look me in the eye."

He was done with his mother. Ryder had other priorities.

"Good-bye."

The door closed with a firm click behind them as they walked out of the hotel suite. Jason remained a silent wall of strength beside him. The whole world had turned on its head with his mother's stunning revelation. And yet…it meant very little to him when he glanced over at Jason, who gripped his hand tighter and gave him a wink. Their marriage had been tested in the most horrific way possible, and they'd come out on the other side of hope and fear, reunited in love and closer than ever.

"Thank you for being here with me. I could never have done this without you by my side."

Facing him with a wicked smile curving his lips,

Jason took him by the shoulder and without a care that they were in a public place, took his mouth in a bruising, possessive kiss. Helpless as always whenever Jason touched him, Ryder dug his hands into Jason's wavy hair and tugged him closer. Their tongues danced and played off each other until Ryder pulled away, panting heavily.

"Not that I'm complaining, but what was that for?"

"If you have to ask, I've been neglecting you." The smile faded from his lips, and Jason leaned his hip against the wall next to Ryder, never taking his eyes from his face. "I'm so proud of how you handled everything in there. You amazed me with your courage and honesty. I know how much you wanted your family reunited. Your whole family. But at least now you know the truth, and you'll always have Landon and your dad."

" 'And the truth shall set you free,' isn't that the saying?" Never had those words more meaning than right now. Finally Ryder had his truth, and it not only set him free, it taught him a lesson. That he was stronger than he thought, and loved more than he imagined.

"It is," said Jason.

"I didn't think it was possible to be happier than when we got married, and then Gemma came along and completed us in a way I didn't even know we were missing. But today, being with you again in your parents' house reaffirmed how it could never be anyone but you for me. I love you."

Jason's arms came around him, drawing him close.

"I feel the same way. I'd never laid eyes on you before the day you rescued those dogs, but the moment I saw you I recognized you. I knew you belonged to me."

Maybe if he and Jason were torn apart the way his mother and Emmaline had been, he too would be unable to recover. Certainly Ryder knew he'd never love anyone again. But to spend your whole life not only being miserable yourself, but causing pain and misery to others through no fault of their own was unfathomable. His mother had said she had no choice; she had to marry whomever her father wanted, and Ryder believed that, especially all those years ago. He wasn't foolish enough to think every marriage made between people of extreme wealth was a love match. But to mourn your entire life away instead of finding common ground with the person you were bound to, or something or someone else to lavish your affection on, seemed nothing less than heartbreaking.

And in his mother's case, futile. For now she had nothing—no children since she'd pushed him and Landon away, and no home, as that designer's paradise of an apartment held no warmth or loving memories. Maybe she and Emmaline would rekindle their relationship, maybe not. In finding his courage he'd released the ties in his mind that still bound him to her.

"Let's go home to Gemma. I need to hold her."

"Yeah," said Jason, that wicked glint returning to his eyes. "And after we hold her, and kiss her, and tell her how much we love her, I'm going to spend the entire night making love to you until you can't walk."

Ryder slung his arm around Jason and pushed the button for the elevator, glancing over his shoulder at the closed door to Emmaline's suite, then put his mother out of his mind.

"Sounds like a damn fine plan to me. Last one in the car sleeps in the wet spot."

Chapter Seventeen

"ARE YOU SURE Ryder's okay? It must've been a tremendous shock to discover a secret like that about his mother."

It had been an exhausting day for them all, and as soon as they came home Ryder went upstairs to see Gemma. After fixing a loose stair railing, Jason had peeked in on them and smiled. The two had fallen asleep curled up next to each other on his and Ryder's bed, Ryder holding Gemma close. On silent tiptoes, Jason backed out of the room and shut the door almost all the way, leaving it open a crack. Something on the stove smelled deliciously like his mother's famous chili-spiced brisket, and Jason's mouth watered as he sauntered into the kitchen and stood behind her. He peered over her shoulder into the pot. Yep. Brisket. Without even asking, he took the spoon from his mother's hand and tasted it.

"That's so good I could eat the entire thing myself."

A pink tinge stained his mother's face at his compliment. "Oh, stop it, silly." Grabbing the spoon back, she fixed him with a pretend glare. "I made this because I know it's Ryder's favorite. The minute you walked in, I could see something traumatic had happened; his eyes looked so sad and dark."

Frowning, Jason leaned against the kitchen counter. "You know Ryder; he'd rather sweep things under the rug. We had a long talk during the car ride home, and he admitted, finally, that hearing his mother say she should never have been a parent shook him." There were things he wouldn't tell his mother, private things, like how he held Ryder through his tears after he admitted how much it hurt to know she'd wanted to terminate her pregnancy, or that she'd never really loved him. Those were personal to them both and would remain in their circle of trust.

"I feel sorry for her." With the meat finished to her satisfaction, she set the heavy lid on the dutch oven and turned down the flame.

"Sorry? For her? She doesn't deserve your pity."

Her brows pinched together, and she frowned. "Of course she does."

"Ma," he said. "She is a cold, heartless person." If he hadn't been talking to his mother, he would've used a harsher word, like bitch. A special place in hell existed for people like Astrid Daniels. "She doesn't deserve one second of your pity."

"Do you want some coffee?" At his nod, she poured him a cup, then pointed to the table. "Sit."

At her gesture, they both took a seat at the oak

kitchen table. "Think about it. Here she has a son who's this wonderful man, a man anyone would be proud to have as their own, yet she couldn't connect with him, or with Landon either. Instead, she's locked herself in this personal hell with no way out."

"She has a way out," said Jason stubbornly. "Apologize to Ryder for the way she's always treated him." In Jason's mind, the indisputable fact remained that Astrid Daniels cared only about herself and no one else.

"It isn't that simple. Look at you. You hold grudges for years over slights from a woman who barely knows you. You and Ryder had issues yourselves because sometimes you can't see someone else's point of view, only your own."

Surprised, Jason wanted to argue with her but found he couldn't. Instead, he looked down into his cup of coffee. "I'm not a bad person. You make it sound like I was the sole cause of our problems." He glanced up at her. "It wasn't only my fault."

Immediately, her expression changed. "Of course not. You're a wonderful husband and father. And you should be sticking up for Ryder like you do. But," she took a sip of her coffee, "you need to understand and listen to what Ryder wants. And if it's working out a relationship with his mother and he's willing to forgive, who are we to tell him no?"

The warm hazelnut smell from the coffee teased his nose, and he took a deep, satisfying drink. "We talked about it already. It's like she resents our happiness because she couldn't have her own, but after the discussion we had with her today, I think Ryder finally saw that. Of course I'd want him to have the same type of relationship with his mother like I have with you. But not everyone gets that."

The best times of his life had been spent at home, laughing around the kitchen table, or on family vacations. Jason planned to emulate the same warmth and love his parents had provided him with his own children. Finding Ryder and falling in love with him hadn't altered those plans; he and Ryder had discussed having children before they got married, and they wanted at least two, maybe more. What Ryder missed growing up—a loving home, family traditions, and acceptance—Jason would make sure he had now as his husband.

"Maybe you need to give it some time. And if it doesn't happen, at least you can always say you tried. But shutting Ryder down isn't the right thing to do."

"I know that now. But he needs to let me know how he feels and stop holding everything inside. I'm not a mind reader."

His mother's face softened, and she put her hand on top of his. "I know you're not. And I'm not criticizing you. I know whatever you've done is out of love for Ryder."

"I don't want to see him hurt anymore."

The overpowering love he had for Ryder enveloped him. Jason needed to make sure tonight Ryder knew how much he was loved. Perhaps his mother sensed the intensity of his feelings because she squeezed his hand, then stood up.

"I'm going to get home. Gemma had a good day and her energy level is certainly coming back."

Relief flooded through Jason. "I know. They told us after the transplant that a month is the benchmark. That once we passed that point we should start seeing improvement. And now that we're at five weeks post-transplant, I understand. A few days ago her eyes seemed so bright and she had that pink in her cheeks I haven't seen in so long."

His mother slipped on her coat and came over to give him a fierce hug.

"She's going to be okay. And so are you and Ryder."

"I know. And I also know I don't tell you enough how much I love you and Dad and appreciate all you've done these past few months."

"You don't thank us. We're your parents; we'd go through hell for you."

Jason hugged her, wishing Ryder could have had the same, hoping what they did have would be enough.

"REMIND ME TO thank your mom for the dinner. It was amazing."

Ryder lay stretched out on the sofa, shoes off, a contented smile on his face. Gemma had felt well enough to join them, and from her animated behavior

Jason knew they'd turned a corner; their little girl would be okay. Sure, there were still checkups and monthly doctor appointments in the foreseeable future, but the yawning black fear that she wouldn't survive had faded to the background. He could only pray it continued and her body wouldn't reject the transplant in the future.

"She loves doing it, and her brisket is the best."

Ryder licked his lips. "Mmm. Don't I know it." His eyelids fluttered shut.

A tug of lust surged through Jason, and he wanted Ryder right then and there. Gemma had already gone to sleep, and the house stood silent. He flicked on the music system he'd installed in the house, and soft jazz purred from the speakers.

"That's nice." Ryder sighed with obvious pleasure and settled more firmly into the cushions. "I thought I'd be more awake since I took that nap before dinner, but I'm still wiped."

Jason took the time to light several candles and dimmed the lamps low. "Remember what I promised earlier? I'm ready. What about you?" While Ryder slept, Jason had prepared the fireplace with fresh kindling and laid out a sheepskin rug they'd bought on a trip to Vermont years ago. He bent over and after starting the fire, placed the decorative gate in front of it, then pulled off his sweatshirt and stepped out of his jeans and boxers, feeling the encroaching heat from the fireplace play over his naked flesh. Low candles sent flickering shadows across Ryder's face, and Jason couldn't hold back a smile when Ryder's eyes opened wide.

"What have you done?" A teasing smile curved his lips. "Don't bother answering. Whatever it is, I know I'm going to like it." He sat up, pulled off his own sweater, and wriggled out of the sweatpants he'd changed into earlier. "We haven't made love down here in a long time." A wistful expression crossed his face. "It reminds me of when we first got married."

Holding out his hand, Jason spoke softly. "Come lie down with me."

Ryder stood and after stepping out of his boxers as well, walked naked toward the fire. Jason couldn't take his eyes off his husband; the firelight glowed over Ryder's skin and golden hair. Heat washed over him that had nothing to do with the fireplace; Jason was transported to when they first met and merely being in the same room with Ryder set his blood burning. His cock ached, and he stroked himself, passing his thumb over the crown to gather the fluid already leaking from the tip.

Never taking his eyes from him, Ryder stood in front of him, his own cock hard, the wide head glistening. "I want you so much."

"You have me, babe. Now, tomorrow. Forever." Jason sank to his knees and took Ryder into his mouth. Ryder moaned low and deep, a sexy, electrifying sound.

"Fuck, Jase, yeah." He planted his feet wide, and Jason eagerly sucked him down, lapping at the tip, swirling his tongue, then taking him down to the root, where he buried his face in the smell of hot skin, warm musk, and desire.

Gliding his fingers down Ryder's trembling thigh, Jason cupped his balls, all the while continuing to suck and lick at Ryder's cock. Ryder rocked his hips, and Jason let his cock glide in and out of his mouth, each time taking it down progressively deeper. It wouldn't be long, Jason knew from experience, loving the clench of Ryder's hands in his hair and hearing Ryder's soft cries urging him on. After inserting a finger in his mouth to pick up some wetness, Jason reached behind Ryder and slid the finger inside Ryder's hole, down to the first knuckle.

"Ahh, fuck me." The grip Ryder had on his hair tightened, and Jason welcomed the pleasure-pain as Ryder thrust himself to the back of Jason's throat and climaxed. Jason swallowed him down, his own body vibrating with need. When Ryder finished pulsing, Jason let him slip from his mouth and sat back on his heels, staring up at Ryder, who stood with a blissed-out smile on his face.

"Mmm. My turn."

He reached for Jason, who batted his hand away. "Nuh-uh. Lie down. I told you." He trailed his fingers up Ryder's thigh, loving the wiry, soft hair and warm skin. "I'm going to pound you so hard you'll feel me for days afterward. If I could leave a piece of me inside you, I would, to let you know you're mine."

"Oh, babe." Ryder sank down to his knees and took

Jason's face between the palms of his hands. "I already have a piece of you with me. Your heart. Remember, I told you it's mine."

They kissed—a glide of lips, a touch of tongues, pressing, slanting, hot and hungry, wet and warm. He couldn't get enough of Ryder's mouth, and he grunted, pushing Ryder down so he lay naked and spread out beneath him.

"Fuck, yeah, you're mine. Don't ever doubt it. Never slip away from me again." He dipped his head down and held Ryder's arms while he proceeded to take him apart piece by piece. Ryder loved having his nipples touched, and Jason nibbled on the hard nubs before sucking each one into his mouth.

"Ahhh, shit." Ryder writhed, but Jason held on to his wrists and kissed his way down Ryder's straining torso. Avoiding Ryder's half-erect cock, Jason licked at his belly button, then across his stomach to his hip bone, leaving a wet trail behind, but not before blowing a stream of cool air over Ryder's skin. It turned him on to see Ryder shiver with anticipation, his long limbs trembling from the effort it took to hold back. The heady scent of Ryder's desire, mingled with the smell of the fire amped up Jason's arousal until he couldn't hold on any longer. He let go of Ryder's knees and pushed them upward, exposing Ryder's ass.

"Fuck, that's hot." Jason spread Ryder apart and dove in, burying his face between Ryder's taut thighs, first spearing his tongue inside Ryder's silky hole, then licking and sucking it, wanting to light up those sensitive nerve endings to drive Ryder wild.

"Oh God," Ryder cried out, arching upward, whimpering, his hands digging into the fur of the sheepskin rug.

"Yeah, feel good, babe? I love your taste, your smell. It drives me wild. I'm gonna eat you up."

The sound of Ryder's moans sent fiery desire pouring through his veins like warm honey, spiking Jason's lust to an almost painful peak. Their need for one another had always been electric, but tonight Jason sensed a shift. Like when they'd first met and fell in love, Jason had to reassure Ryder how much he meant to him. Words didn't come as easily to him as they did to Ryder, so Jason had to show him with his body what he held so deep and strong within his heart. The touch of Ryder's hand across the sheets, the curve of his lips at a joke, the slow pulse of hunger when their bodies joined together—everything about Ryder fed his soul and gave him life.

"I want you," said Ryder through gritted teeth. And Jason had no doubts, sitting back on his heels to study Ryder's face flushed from heat, passion, or both. His hair lay in sweaty strands across his forehead, and his eyes blazed with an emotion Jason hadn't seen in months. "I need you, Jase."

And nothing else would ever matter but those words between them. He slicked his cock up with lube, never taking his eyes off his husband, knowing how lucky they were. Sliding inside Ryder's heat, Jason bent low so their damp foreheads touched, and whispered, "I need you too. I love you."

Ryder rocked his hips upward, locking his ankles around Jason's back, thrusting against Jason's cock deep inside him. Nothing compared to being inside Ryder; the slow, sensual drag of hot, naked skin against skin, the push and pull, all that hard, delicious friction sent wave after wave of pulsing sensation over Jason until the clench of tight muscle on his fevered, aching flesh shattered his core, drenching him in its sweetness.

Pleasure burst over him, and he clutched Ryder's sweat-slicked shoulders, barely able to breathe. A quiet sob escaped him while tremors wracked his limbs. Tonight had gone beyond lovemaking; tonight he'd surrendered to Ryder, given himself up without a thought. He lay on top of Ryder, sated and drained.

A few minutes later he pulled out but held on to Ryder, whispering in his ear and not letting him move.

"I remember the first time we kissed, the first time you touched me. You were never a stranger. We'd been reunited after a long journey away from each other."

Like all those years ago, he pressed his lips to Ryder's, their softness a familiar pathway to his heart. They'd survived family heartbreak, the devastating pain of their child's illness, and the hazards and struggles of life getting in the way. Doubt had crept in, but both he and Ryder, holding on to the strength of their love, refused to allow it to take root and fester.

“I haven’t forgotten.” Ryder gazed at him, his eyes soft and luminous in the firelight. “I remember everything about you: the way your eyes light up when you’re happy, the smell of your skin and how you taste.”

They remained holding each other, the snapping of the wood in the fireplace a comforting sound.

With regret, Jason stood, and Ryder followed, grimacing.

“I need to shower and clean up.”

“Go on, I’ll take care of the fireplace.”

After collecting his clothes, Ryder went upstairs, and Jason banked the fire, making sure the fireproof gate sat securely in front of the hearth. He picked up his belongings and blew out the candles, then trod silently up the steps. The shower still ran, so Jason slipped on a pair of sweatpants and went to check on Gemma. She lay in her bed, curled up in a ball, and Jason wondered if he’d ever again watch her sleep without checking to see if she still breathed.

“Thank you, God,” he whispered in the hush of the room.

“It takes a scare to learn priorities, huh?”

Ryder slipped his arms around him, smelling fantastic from his shower, and Jason wondered if he could be enticed to take another one. With him.

“My priority is you and our daughter. And Ry?” Ryder nuzzled at his neck, and Jason knew his chance at that shower and whatever else happened was guaranteed.

“Hmm, yeah?” The feel of Ryder’s lips on his neck

had him instantly hard and aching.

"If you want to use your trust-fund money for Gemma's school, I'm fine with that."

"What made you change your mind?"

"Life is too fucking short to waste. If I have anything that can make life easier for us, I'd be stupid not to use it, you know? If I don't have to work so hard and can be home for dinner now with you and Gem, I'm not gonna screw that up. Not again."

"Yeah." Ryder drew him close and shut Gemma's door behind them. "I think you made a wise decision." He flattened Jason against the wall, the full weight of his erect cock heavy against Jason's thigh. "I knew I married a smart guy."

Cracking a smile, Jason reached behind and pinched Ryder's ass. "I'm full of wise decisions. Like I decided you need to help me wash behind my ears."

Ryder chuckled and kissed him until his head spun and he could barely remember his name.

Chapter Eighteen

One Month Later

GEMMA'S BIRTHDAY PARTY was in full swing when Ryder and Jason snuck away to the kitchen. Jason's parents had sent a text that they'd arrived, and Ryder and Jason needed them to take the video.

"Here, guys. I think they know something's up. I've never seen them so excited."

Both Trouper and Pearl whined and danced at his and Jason's feet. To calm them both, he sank to his knees and looped an arm around their necks.

"You need to be gentle, now. No jumping on her, okay?" He glanced up at Jason. "They're both so good; I think they really understand, don't you?"

"Yeah," said Jason, his face alight with happiness. "I can't wait to see Gemma's face when they come in."

The dogs bathed his face with their tongues and stood quietly now at his feet. Jason held Trouper's leash, and he had Pearl's. It had been almost three months since she'd seen her doggies face-to-face, and Gemma had stopped asking when they were coming home. The doctor had given clearance for them to return, with the caution to try to limit their exposure. There'd be no sleeping in her bed or face-licking, and Gemma would have to wash her hands every time she played with them, but Ryder knew all that was merely incidental to the joy of having the dogs back home with them.

"Ready to see your girl?"

Pearl whined, and Ryder walked out to the living room where everyone else waited. The entire family knew they were surprising Gemma with the return home of her dogs for the first time since she'd been sick. Everyone was there. Liam and Courtney came with baby TJ, and Mark and Julie surprised them all by announcing their engagement, though Ryder knew his mother-in-law had been hoping to add Julie to the family. Nicole and Jessie had made a special trip in for the weekend, and Ryder looked forward to seeing how Jessie and Landon would act toward each other. They'd dated on and off since high school, but Ryder knew Landon wanted to take it to the next level with Jason's youngest sister and date her exclusively. From the way they'd been attached at the hip, concentrating only on each other since Landon had picked her up at Grand Central, it looked like Jessie was all in with that plan. Of course Emily and Connor, their son, Jack, and baby Isabel were there. Their babysitter, Erica, had come with Shanice, and Ryder almost cried as the two little girls hugged each other and started playing as if the past several months hadn't even happened.

"Gem. Look who came to wish you a happy birthday."

"My doggies! Pearl and Trouper!" Gemma left the pile of Legos she, Shanice, and Jack had been playing with. She sprinted across the room, her dress a bright cobalt-blue flash, to fling herself upon them.

"Doing good, you two." Ryder and Jason grinned over their daughter and the dogs. They knew how much the dogs wanted to bark and jump, but they were too well trained to break form. Gemma didn't care and hugged them over and over again.

"I missed you so much. Daddy Ry, are they back to stay? Please?" Her blue eyes filled with tears. "I want them to stay."

"Yes, honey girl. They're back for good. No sleeping in your bed or face-licking though, okay? And you have to wash every time you play with them."

With an unusually solemn face, Gemma nodded. "I promise. I don't ever want them to go away again."

Now that the initial tumult over their return had subsided, he and Jason unsnapped the dogs' leashes and let them off to wander the house. Arms around each other's waists, he and Jason stood and laughed as Pearl and Trouper inspected every piece of furniture, snuffling at the cushions, greeting each person with a lick, and getting scratches and pets.

"We'll have to be careful about our nightly activity now that they're back," Jason murmured in his ear. "I don't need an eighty-pound dog jumping on my back when I'm on top of you."

They'd made it a habit to make love by the fireplace after Gemma went to bed, creating their own little hideaway. Grinning, Ryder kissed Jason's cheek. "I think we can manage to make love on the bed as well as the rug, don't you?"

Desire glowed in Jason's dark-blue eyes. "I could make love to you anywhere. And everywhere. My trailer, the kitchen table, the shower. It's not the place, it's you."

"Okay, you two, break it up." Connor snapped his fingers in front of their faces, and Ryder's face heated. "This is a PG party, and the looks between you were definitely R-rated, maybe even X."

Of course it would be Connor who gave them shit, but he shouldn't be surprised. His best friend lived for moments like this. Letting go of Jason, Ryder hugged Connor close. "If we haven't said it already, thank you. You and Emily…" Emotion got the better of him for the moment, and he choked up. "We couldn't have gotten to this day without you two." Keeping his arm firmly around Connor's shoulder, Ryder raised his voice to address the crowd.

"Jason and I want to thank everyone here today. Without your help I know we couldn't have made it through. Nothing prepares you for illness. But when the illness is your child's…" His voice caught and trembled. Would there ever come a time when his voice wouldn't betray him?

"Daddy Ry, don't cry." Gemma tugged at his pants, and he picked her up, holding her close, loving her sweetness. "I'm okay, I promise."

"I know, baby girl. I'm crying 'cause I'm happy. Grown-ups do that a lot."

His father appeared at his side with Denise. "Looking at her, I see you as a child. You and Landon. I'm so proud of you and Jason; not only for the men you are but the parents you've become."

"Hug." Gemma held out her arms to Denise, who scooped her up and held her tight as Ryder gave his father a hug of his own.

"Thanks, Dad. We couldn't have done it without you and Denise. Gemma loves you guys so much."

"So," his father said, blue eyes twinkling, "I can finally take this off, then?" He held up his hand to show the sparkly nail polish he wore.

"Grandpa. You still have your sparkle nails. Me too." Gemma held out her hands. "Don't take it off."

"I can't believe it." With wonder, Ryder gazed down at his father's perfectly manicured hands. "I thought you meant it as a silly, one-day promise."

"It might have started out that way, but I watched a video of a man whose daughter painted his nails, and he wore it with such pride I thought to myself, why not? It's for Gemma." He reached over and smoothed her hair. "I'd do anything for her."

Tears spilled over, and Ryder brushed them away. "I love you, Dad. I'm sorry it took so long for everything to work out between us."

"It was worth waiting for. And I'm finally happy. Did you know I had a long talk with your mother last week?"

Startled, Ryder glanced over at Jason who raised his brows in surprise, then returned to focus on his father. "Uh, no. We haven't had any contact since that day Jason and I met with her."

"I'm sure you know the story, then." He turned to Denise and murmured in her ear. Giving them a sympathetic look, Denise carried Gemma back to the party and the other guests. Everyone crowded around her, and for a moment Ryder's heart sped up with anxiety that it was too much, too soon. Helen, quick to take charge, had Denise sit next to her, and everyone else moved back a bit. With a sigh of relief, Ryder turned back to his father.

"Emmaline?"

At his father's nod, a wave of pity rolled over Ryder. "I feel so sorry for you, Dad. We both do." At Jason's nod, he continued. "I can't imagine how hard it was to live like that, knowing Mother never wanted you near her."

"It doesn't excuse my neglect, but I did selfishly stay away, knowing I wasn't wanted. At least now we both have what we've always wanted. I have my children and a wife who loves me, and your mother has the only person she's ever loved." His eyes dimmed for a moment. "My biggest regret is that you and Landon had to suffer because of our mistakes. Back when we got married there were no such things as prenuptial agreements, and a divorce would have been a huge scandal and cost so much. That's no excuse now, but all I can do is try and be here for you boys today. Your mother and I stayed together for the wrong reasons and should have separated years earlier."

"We both got a raw deal, but no regrets, Dad. This is a party and a house that celebrates life—never more so than today. We all make choices, and Mother made hers."

He and Jason, along with his father, walked into the living room, and Ryder couldn't help but smile at the chaotic scene. Jack sat next to Gemma and Shanice, directing Liam, Mark, Landon, and the other adults on the right way to build a Lego spaceship. The two dogs lay behind Gemma on either side, their tails wagging and eyes bright. If dogs could look happy, Pearl and Trouper were ecstatic.

"It's a beautiful sight, isn't it? What I always wanted. A home filled with family, friends, and love." Jason squeezed him around the waist, catching a quick kiss. "You made it all possible. Listening to your father talk about how hard he worked and how he missed your childhood, I'm never going to allow that to happen. All I want is right here, right in front of me."

"Same. And maybe another baby? We could speak to Shannon and see if she's willing to be a surrogate again. What do you say?"

"Yeah?" Jason's broad smile matched his own. "I think that's great. Gemma could use a little brother or sister."

The doorbell rang, and Ryder checked his watch. "Must be the pizzas we ordered. I'll get it." With a lightness in his step he hadn't had in months, Ryder fished in his back pocket for his wallet with one hand while he opened the door with the other.

"Hey, that was fast. We only ordered…"

His voice trailed away. Standing on his front porch were his mother and Emmaline. A frozen half smile rested on his mother's lips, yet it couldn't hide the fear in her eyes, which proved shocking.

"Ryder. May we come in?"

Ryder didn't know whether to laugh or cry. In the end, he gave up and went with what was in his heart.

"Why are you here? I thought we said everything the last time we met."

Emmaline's hand rested on his mother's shoulder and gave it a gentle squeeze. "Go ahead, Astrid."

Filled with confusion, Ryder glanced from one to the other. "Go ahead and what? What could you possibly say that would change anything?"

Footsteps sounded in the background, and Ryder instinctively knew it was Jason. He braced himself for the inevitable uproar.

"Babe, what happened? I thought you ran…" Jason stopped short, wide-eyed. "What's going on?"

Jason's appearance grounded him, giving him the

presence of mind to collect his thoughts and stay strong.

"My mother and Emmaline showed up. They were about to tell me why."

"Aren't you going to ask us inside? I'd like to see my granddaughter."

"That's our decision. Why are you here, Mother? Answer me that."

Drawing her coat closer to her thin frame, his mother shivered slightly. "I owe you an apology. You and Mr. Mallory—*Jason*—both. It was wrong of me to be harsh and cruel to you that day in Emmaline's suite. But I'm not asking you to forgive my behavior toward you. And I meant what I said when I told you I never should have had children."

"You know, Mother, if you're trying out for the worst apology of the year award, I think you'll win hands down." Ryder leaned into Jason's warmth and folded his arms. "Go on, though. We're listening."

She blinked, looking disconcerted for a moment, then straightened her shoulders and began again. "But your daughter doesn't know me like that. And you were right when you said she's entitled to her family. Will you let me be a part of her life, myself and Emmaline?"

If his life had depended on it, Ryder never would have imagined this day would come to pass. "You want to be a part of Gemma's life?"

A nod. "If you'll allow us. I promise to accept your husband and your marriage, though I doubt he'd ever believe me."

About to answer, Ryder caught himself and dragged

Jason out of earshot of his mother and Emmaline. "What do you think?" he murmured. "We can make an excuse and send them away."

Jason's dark-blue eyes warmed with an inner glow. "Let's not be so hasty. Maybe we should let them in."

"What?" Ryder replied with an astonished sputter. "Are you serious?" He wasn't foolish enough to think he and his mother would ever be friends, but this tentative outreach…

"Yeah. If not for your mother, Gemma might not be here. And like you've said, don't live with regrets. We have everything we want, and she has nothing. Let our daughter have a chance with her as a grandmother, what you couldn't have with her as a mother."

Jason's warm, calloused hand stroked his face, and Ryder soaked in his familiar touch, the one he craved every day of his life. They kissed, and the touch of Jason's lips imprinted itself in the pulse of his blood through his veins and every beat of his heart. Forever.

"You're an amazing man, and every day together proves how lucky I am you're mine." With one final kiss to Jason's palm, Ryder faced his mother and swung the door open wide.

"Come inside. Welcome to our home."

The End

Join my newsletter to get access to get first looks at WIP, exclusive content, contests, deleted scenes and much more! Never any spam.
Newsletter: http://bit.ly/FelicesNewsletter

About the Author

I have always been a romantic at heart. I believe that while life is tough, there is always a happy ending around the corner, My characters have to work for it, however. Like life in NYC, nothing comes easy and that includes love.

I live in New York City with my husband and two children and hopefully soon a cat of my own. My day begins with a lot of caffeine and ends with a glass or two of red wine. I practice law but daydream of a time when I can sit by a beach somewhere and write beautiful stories of men falling in love. Although there are bound to be a few bumps along the way, a Happily Ever After is always guaranteed.

Website:

www.felicestevens.com

Facebook:

facebook.com/felice.stevens.1

Twitter:

twitter.com/FeliceStevens1

Goodreads:

goodreads.com/author/show/8432880.Felice_Stevens

Other titles by Felice Stevens

Through Hell and Back Series:

A Walk Through Fire

After the Fire—Coming February 2017

Embrace the Fire—Coming March 2017

The Memories Series:

Memories of the Heart

One Step Further

The Greatest Gift

The Breakfast Club Series:

Beyond the Surface

Betting on Forever

Second to None

What Lies Between Us

A Holiday to Remember

A Rescued Heart Series:

Rescued

Reunited

Other:

Learning to Love

The Arrangement

Please Don't Go

CPSIA information can be obtained
at www.ICGtesting.com
Printed in the USA
BVHW040531250420
578479BV00010B/921

9 781542 788793